Money, Murder & Memories 3

Lock Down Publications and Ca$h
Presents

Money, Murder & Memories 3

A Novel by *Malik D. Rice*

Lock Down Publications
P.O. Box 944
Stockbridge, Ga 30281

Copyright 2020 by Malik D. Rice
Money, Murder & Memories 3

First Edition May 2021
Printed in the United States of America

Lock Down Publications
Like our page on Facebook: Lock Down Publications @
www.facebook.com/lockdownpublications.ldp
Cover design and layout by: **Dynasty Cover Me**
Book interior design by: **Shawn Walker**
Edited by: **Shamika Smith**

Malik D. Rice

Stay Connected with Us!

Text **LOCKDOWN** to 22828 to stay up-to-date with new releases, sneak peaks, contests and more…

Thank you!

Submission Guideline.

Submit the first three chapters of your completed manuscript to ldpsubmissions@gmail.com, subject line: Your book's title. The manuscript must be in a .doc file and sent as an attachment. Document should be in Times New Roman, double spaced and in size 12 font. Also, provide your synopsis and full contact information. If sending multiple submissions, they must each be in a separate email.

Have a story but no way to send it electronically? You can still submit to LDP/Ca$h Presents. Send in the first three chapters, written or typed, of your completed manuscript to:

LDP: Submissions Dept
P.O. Box 944
Stockbridge, Ga 30281

DO NOT send original manuscript. Must be a duplicate.

Provide your synopsis and a cover letter containing your full contact information.

Thanks for considering LDP and Ca$h Presents.

Malik D. Rice

Chapter 1

Gucci paced her bathroom floor, thinking about a number of things. She was excited because she was sure that the outcome would tip in her favor this time. She finally stopped walking, sent a quick prayer up to her ancestors, and then picked up the pregnancy test from off the sink counter. She took a deep breath and looked down at the plastic stick in her hand. There was only one line showing, so the results were negative and that meant she wasn't pregnant.

"God damnnnn, bruh!" She threw the stick at the wall before plopping down on the edge of the toilet with her face in her hands.

She'd been trying to trap Donny with a baby for some time now. It's been three months since she'd convinced him to start fucking her without a condom, and she still wasn't getting pregnant. She was starting to believe that it was something wrong with her, so she planned on visiting a doctor to check her out. She could feel Donny's interest for her fading away, so she had to do something quickly.

***

Donny sat up in his bed, making future plans with Hennessey. They'd just found out that she was four months pregnant with a little baby boy. He wasn't planning on having a child this early, but he definitely wasn't complaining. He was young and rich. Why not?

"So, how you want to play it? You know I can't leave this house," said Donny.

Hennessey sighed. "Marley's alright, but I refuse to let my child grow up under the same roof as Jay's evil ass."

"It's not just your child, it's *our* child, and Jay's really not all that bad. He's really a funny ass nigga, and he's actually good with kids for your information," he informed matter-a-factly.

Hennessey gave him a knowing look. "Our son will live with me in Miami, and you can come to visit on the weekends, or whatever works for you."

Donny leaned down and gave her a kiss on the lips. "Don't be like that, baby girl. I'm gon' be in y'all lives regardless. What Demy have to say about this?" He was curious to know.

"She just called me all kinds of stupid because I've been turning down all types of men for you."

"Damnnn, she's hating on a young nigga like that?" he asked with a slight mug.

Hennessey shook her head no. "No, it's not like that. She just wants the best for me, and she knows I'm not your top priority that's all."

"She acts like I'm forcing you to be with me or something. I be telling you that you could do better all the time."

Hennessey looked up at him amusingly. "I think that's what gets her the most. You got all of me, and there's nothing anyone can do about it because I love it here," she admitted before leaning up and kissing his soft lips.

***

Jay and Marley had basically become Siamese twins over the past few months. They'd become the driving force behind Donny. Together, they did some major damage, and everyone knew it. They sat in the living room playing *Call of Duty* online, enjoying their downtime when Donny interrupted.

"Aye, we got a problem y'all," he informed while walking into the kitchen and pulling his t-shirt over his head.

Jay paused the game and turned around. "Wassup?"

"I don't want to repeat myself. I'm gon' tell everybody when we get next door." Donny informed.

A few minutes later, they were all gathered in Dizzy's backyard. The sun was shining harder than usual, but Dizzy had a big tent put up so he could kick it in his backyard on days like this.

He was halfway asleep when Donny called his phone, telling him that he was in the backyard waiting for him. "What's so important? You must've got word from Rondo about something."

"Come on, bruh." Donny gave Dizzy a knowing look. "You know ain't nobody heard from that nigga. We hear all his words through Manny.

This ain't got nothing to do with him though. I called this lil' meeting because we might have a problem on our hands."

Dizzy, Jay, and Marley were all ears. They didn't say a word, just sat patiently and waited for Donny to continue.

"Alright, look... I just got word from this lil' Crip hoe that Antonio be fuckin' with. She told me that they having a lil' civil war on that side. A nigga named Falcon is going up against Cleezy for his spot over the city."

Dizzy shrugged his shoulders hard. "So! Fuck that got to do with us? We DG."

"Yeah, we are DG, but it also got something to do with us because of the reason that they're going at it."

Malik D. Rice

Chapter 2

Gino might not have been at the top of the food chain, but he definitely was up in the ranks and was satisfied with his slice of the pie. He took pride in being Donny's head enforcer. All he had to do was make sure the Mafiosos paid their dues, and get the money dropped off for Donny. That only took one day out of the week, so that gave him six days out of the week to focus on his own steadily growing empire. He now had ten soldiers of his own that were down to follow his every command.

He was a Mafioso, so that gave him the freedom to operate his own business, and like always, he was in the business of taking. It was in his blood. The only difference is that he was thinking bigger, way bigger.

He walked into Simon G Jewelry, one of Charlotte's finest jewelry stores.

Boom!

He fired off a warning shot with his Mossberg 500 that blew a big hole into the ceiling. "Let me see them muthafuckin' hands! Any heroes *will* die today!"

There were two armed security guards at the entrance that were being zip-tied by two of Gino's soldiers, and three jewelry salesmen that were working the showroom floor. Two more of the soldiers gathered up the salesmen, while Gino headed to the back with, Danger, hot on his heels. They passed the bathroom and the lunchroom and headed straight towards the office at the far end of the hallway.

Boc!

An elder Jewish woman fired a shot at Gino with her .22 revolver, but unfortunately for her, she missed.

Boc!

Danger leaned into the room, and fired a hallow tip, from his .45, but he didn't miss. He struck the owner in her right shoulder, causing her to fall backward, off of her chair, onto the floor.

"Ahhhhhhhhhh-ha-ahhhh! Please, please, please, please don't kill meee! There's a lot of money and over two million dollars' worth of jewelry in the safe! Take it all!" she pleaded hysterically in between sobs.

"Open it!" Gino barked, causing her to jump.

She didn't waste her time crawling over to the safe and opening it up for them. "That's everything."

Gino crashed the butt of his gun into her head, knocking her out instantly before helping Danger unload the safe. She was right, the safe was *loaded*.

***

Nobody in their crew breathed easy until they made it back to Fayetteville inside of their safehouse, right off of Murchison Road.

Gino and Danger dropped off the five soldiers, who attended the lick with them, and assured them that they would receive their cut soon.

They stood up, staring down at the contents on the table. This was the biggest lick either one of them had ever pulled. A huge pile of hundreds sat on one of the tables, and a nice pile of jewelry sat on the other end.

"We gon' have to be careful trying to move this shit. That's a lot of jewelry," Danger advised. "Ain't no telling who was invested into that store, or whose protection they were up under."

Gino was in deep thought. "We can pay Donny and the soldiers with the jewelry we got off the showroom floor and the cash from the safe. You and I can just split what we make off the jewelry from the safe. I know we can at least sell that shit for half of what it's worth."

Danger extended his arm, draped it across Gino's shoulder, and drew him close. He kissed Gino on the top of his head. "I love you, lil' nigga. You just like me, but ten times better, and I'm proud of you. You gon' be one of the greats."

Before he went to prison, he didn't show Gino too much affection. However, while he was in prison, he vowed to do so when he made it out. He also vowed to follow his son to the end of the earth, and that's exactly what he was doing.

Gino and Danger pulled up to Donny's spot and found him lounging in his driveway, washing his jet-black Ferrari. He had his shirt off, jewelry on, and music blasting.

"Who this nigga think he is?" Gino asked jokingly. He looked up to and respected Donny. He was honored to be working for him. He'd proven himself to be a great leader over time. Manny was right to glorify him as much as he did.

Danger shrugged. "Looks like a successful ass young nigga to me, just enjoying life."

"But ain't the FEDs still around? Why would he buy that new car? I know it cost a couple hundred thousand," Gino inquired.

"Yeah, but what's the point in getting all this money if you can't spend it? Fuck the FEDs."

Gino nodded his head. "I can go for that. Shit, that's how I'm feeling."

"Yeah, but he got legit money behind him, so he can do that. You can't." Danger informed matter-a-factly, raining on his parade.

Donny looked their way but went back to washing his car. A few seconds later, Marley got out of the driver's seat of the car and made his way down the driveway towards them.

"Y'all must got an emergency? Because y'all definitely know better than to pull up unexpected," Marley scolded, after Gino rolled the passenger's window down for him.

"We just hit a big lick. I just came to drop Donny's cut off personally," Gino informed while holding up the black North Face book bag.

"Come on, man! Y'all tripping. Go give the money to Gucci like you give everything else. We can't be caught making no exchanges," Marley spat while looking around cautiously. "How much is it anyway, so I can tell Donny?"

"A hundred thousand and some jewelry," Gino answered after sitting the bag back on the floor.

"Aight, go take it to Gucci. I'll let Donny know... Y'all stay on point too, we might have to ride on some shit soon."

Gino leaned closer. "What happened? Just let me know. We'll go handle that shit right now!"

Marley shook his head. "Nah, just chill. We got to play this smart. We'll be in touch."

"Aight. Just tell Donny not to hesitate to hit my line. Me and mines are always ready," Gino assured before Danger swerved off.

"What the hell they want?" asked Donny when Marley got back in the car.

"They just hit a lick and came to give you your cut... A hundred thousand and some jewelry," Marley informed before picking his phone up out of the cupholder.

Donny leaned into the car, with a raised brow. "Damn! Who the fuck they hit? If they kicking me that much, it must've been a major lick."

"I know right. That's what I was thinking, but they didn't say, and I didn't ask. I was just trying to get their hot asses off our doorstep."

Donny smirked. "I really don't give a damn. They did the right thing and gave me my cut. I don't care who they take it off of, as long as they pay taxes," he stated, before squatting back down to finish polishing his black rims.

Chapter 3

At one point in time, Antonio said that he would never leave The Chase no matter how much money he made. He actually felt that way when he had said it, but time brings change, and he eventually outgrew his hood. Two months ago, he purchased a newly built townhouse on the upper east side. It was an upscale neighborhood and a long way from the trailer park. He loved it.

He stood in the doorway of his front door and watched as a blue Mercedes Benz E-Class pulled up into his driveway. A bright yellow Amazonian woman got out of the driver's seat, looking like a supermodel in her designer threads and big Gucci shades. Her name was Tirasia, and she was quickly falling in love with Antonio's fine ass.

"Why you out here showing off all my goodies?" she asked jealously, as she walked up the walkway towards the doorway, staring at a shirtless, Antonio.

Antonio let her in the house and closed the door behind her. "I can't vibe with these boujie bitches out here, so you really ain't got shit to worry about."

"What about all of them model bitches you working with now?" Tirasia asked with a hand on her hip, looking at him expectantly.

About the same time that Antonio decided to move out of The Chase, Manny launched a modeling agency called YF Beauty. There were six females on the roster, and he ended up convincing Antonio to be the first male model in the company. He made Antonio vow to leave the streets alone and signed him for a $400,000 advance. The rest was history.

Antonio couldn't help but laugh at her jealous ways because she literally had no reason to be. "I mean, I fucked a few of them, but nothing serious. Why you be doing that shit though? You a bad bitch with a lot going on for yourself. Any nigga would be lucky to have you, shawty. You need to start acting like it."

"Oh, you want me to start acting like I don't care, like you?" she asked sassily.

Antonio sighed and chuckled again before walking her over to the couch. "Listen, all I'm saying is that you should work on that shit. That's how you ran your ex off. The type of niggas that you're into needs a confident woman, not an insecure little girl," he advised bluntly.

Tirasia sat there with an open mouth and hurt feelings, then suddenly closed her mouth while making a pouty crybaby face. "Fuck you!" she spat softly.

"Awwww! Come here sexy mammaaaaa." He wrapped his arms around her tightly, even though she resisted.

"No, get off of me with your mean ass! You're right though. Maybe I might need to start fucking with different types of niggas because I'll be damned if I keep letting y'all walk all over my damn feelings," she considered seriously.

Antonio let her go and fell into more laughter. "Yeah, fuckin' right! Yo' ass loves this shit deep down... Anyway, wassup with that nigga Falcon? You got the M.O. on that nigga yet?"

Tirasia rolled her eyes, then nodded her head up and down. "Yup! It's gon' take me some time, but I'll get the drop on his ass. Anyway, while you got me out here on 007 missions and shit, you need to be paying me," she spat with her hand out.

Antonio removed one of the solitary-diamond choke chains from around his neck and laid it in her hand, after removing the YF pendant. "There you go. More than enough."

***

Persia was at the Walgreen's on Bragg Boulevard, sending some money to her aunt through Western Union. It was a hot day, and she was just ready to get back to Tadoe's house to lay up with her man under the coolness of the air conditioner. After sending the money, she decided to grab a few extra hygiene items since she was running out of necessary items at his house.

"I've been waiting to catch yo' lil' ass somewhere by yourself. I wasn't even about to come in this muthafucka, but look at God!" Dizzy joked seriously, as he walked down the aisle with pure infatuation in his eyes. He'd been secretly daydreaming of Persia since he saw her four months ago at Sasha's house.

Persia quickly turned to see who was speaking to her and was met face-to-face with Dizzy. She'd heard about him and had seen him around in passing, but this was her first time being this close up to him.

"I didn't know you believed in God," she countered swiftly, before turning her attention back onto the items on the shelf.

Dizzy took two steps closer, now invading her personal space. "If you believe in the Devil, you got to believe in God. There's no one without the other."

She wasn't expecting an answer like that from him. She looked back up at him and couldn't help but smell the smooth cologne that oozed off of him. *Oh, shitttt! I got to get away from this man,* she thought as she felt her own clit swell.

"Have a nice day, Dizzy," she spat, before storming off, empty-handed. She wasn't even worried about the hygiene on the shelf. She could get it from somewhere else, but right then and there, she had to get away from him.

Dizzy leaned on the shelf with an evil smirk etched on his face, as he watched her little ass jiggle through the pink sundress she wore. "That boy, Tadoe better watch out. That bitch can get got," he boasted to himself.

Malik D. Rice

Chapter 4

Falcon was the best type of individual. That is if he considered you as a friend. But if he saw you as an opposition, it was sure to be a living nightmare for you until you disappeared. In that sense, he was the worst.

He was a legend back in California where he made his name for being ruthless and manipulative. The big-big homies used him for delicate missions such as this one. Cleezy thought that Falcon was just randomly trying to take his spot on the throne, but the reality of the situation was that they sent him out there to overthrow Cleezy because he was losing control of the city. Falcon was there to restore everything that the Crips in Fayetteville had lost.

He'd only been in Fayetteville for three short months and already had built a decent little army of his own, on top of the five soldiers he originally flew out there with. Most of the north side was already his, and once he exterminated, Cleezy, and his lieutenants, the rest of the north side and the entire westside would be his. Then, he could execute his attack on Dilluminati accordingly.

He was currently standing in an empty parking lot, looking down into the trunk of an old car. A fat teenage boy wiggled around in the trunk, struggling to break free of the bondagés that held him together. He looked up at Falcon with pleading eyes.

"Rip that tape off of his mouth," Falcon commanded and watched as one of his men did the deed. "What's yo' name lil' nigga?"

"T-t-tito! Don't whack me, bruh! Don't whack me! Please! I'm just a small fry. I don't hold *no* weight out here. I'm a nobody in the hood," the youngin pleaded desperately while looking up at Falcon. The sun was shining hard, so he couldn't actually see Falcon's face. He could only see his pants and his fat belly, poking up under his Ralph Lauren t-shirt.

Falcon continued to peer down at Tito as he decided what he wanted to do with the lil' nigga. He could literally smell his fear rising up from the trunk, and it fueled his pride. He was grateful to have gotten the drop on the young nigga, and who he had ties with. If he played his cards right, he could be a valuable asset.

"I'm not going to whack you as of right now. Do you know why I had you snatched up? Do you know who I am?" Falcon asked.

Tito shook his head from side to side frantically.

"You better think harder than that, and I'm Falcon Loc, in case you didn't know."

A flash of recognition popped up in Tito's eyes, upon hearing Falcon's name. "It got to be because of my cousin, Blu. That's the only thing that makes sense... If that's the case, then you wasting your time because he's not going to pay too much to get me back," Tito informed matter-a-factly, hoping that it convinced Falcon to cut him loose.

"Nah, I don't want a ransom. I need eyes on the inside to stay ahead of them niggas. You'll get paid for your information, and you'll get to keep your life."

Tito weighed his options inwardly. You'd be surprised what kind of deals a muthafucka would agree to while being held hostage in a rusty trunk. "I got you, just let me out this trunk."

Falcon closed the trunk and walked over to his right-hand man, X, who stood a few feet away in the distance. "You think we can trust this lil' nigga?"

"Not at all, but I think the money will keep the lil' nigga in our pocket because he obviously ain't getting none from the other side. He probably a fuck up, and that's why Blu don't fuck with his ass," said X with his thick arms folded across his chest.

Falcon shrugged his shoulders. "Tell them to take the lil' nigga back where they got him when the sun goes back down and slide him $2,500 just to show him the money ain't a problem." He decided before walking towards his car across the lot.

***

"Man, how the fuck am I gon' tell you some shit I don't know? Shit is real organized out here right now and he knows y'all are watching, so ain't too many slip-ups. Y'all know what the fuck Donny is doing out here. Why y'all don't just lock that nigga up and leave me alone?" Rod asked sourly. He was already mad that he was in bed with the pigs. He fought hard daily not to feel like the scum of the earth.

About six weeks ago, he got caught red-handed making a big sell to some undercover DEA agents, and his whole world flipped. He was brought to an interrogation room downtown where he was presented with *the second chance of a lifetime.*

They made it clear that Donny was their main focus, and he could remain a free man if he acted as their private eyes inside of the organization. He was looking at a minimum of twenty years in a federal prison if he didn't take the deal, but he didn't budge at first.

They let him sit in the interrogation room for a few more hours to think if Donny was worth the sacrifice. During that time, flashbacks of Donny's public assault on him played in his head. He still hadn't recovered from that humiliation. Donny made him shit on himself and his family had to see him like that. He'd be damned if he had to go through the humiliation of them seeing him lose his life in a courtroom.

"Roderick, I'm going to need you to come up with some type of plan to incriminate that little bastard. The big bosses are putting pressure on us to bring him down, so we're putting pressure on you. You need to uphold your end of the bargain and help us bring him down," his handler, Craig, said sternly. He was a clean-cut African American dude who despised street niggas because they felt that they were special. But to him, they weren't, and he vowed to prove it as much as he could.

Rod sighed heavily and ran a hand down his face before looking out of the passenger's window at the passing pedestrians in the parking lot. He was sitting in Craig's Tahoe in the parking lot of a big plaza on Bragg Boulevard. "Donny's a young nigga, but he ain't stupid. He isolated the fuck out of himself and tightened up his circle. He barely shows his face anymore, and he don't touch shit. Why y'all don't just send in an agent undercover? Your case would be stronger that way. I'll give him the game and point him in the right direction."

Craig turned and gave him a stupid look. "Not a chance. For one, an agent can't put in the type of work required to be trusted by Donny, and secondly, it's no secret how you guys treat outsiders out here. My superiors would never sign off on that. It's too much that could go wrong.

That's why we look for cracks in the armor... You're a crack, Rod. You need to spread, so we can break some shit."

Chapter 5

Donny raced through traffic in his new Ferrari. It was as quick and smooth as he anticipated. He had one of DG Rell's songs blasting, and he was booted up off the molly. He was on top of the world and he felt good, which is why he was on his current mission.

He ended up swerving to a stop in the mall's parking lot near the entrance and waited for his men to catch up. He opened the car door, placed one foot onto the pavement outside, turned the music up louder, and started rolling a joint of purple haze. The three trucks that followed behind, caught up eventually. Jay and Marley in one truck, Gino and Danger in another, and Gino's men in the last one.

"You breaching the fuck out of security right now! How the hell are we supposed to protect you with you doing shit like this, nigga? You got on half a million dollars' worth of jewelry with yo' crazy ass!" Marley shouted over the music.

Donny pointed at the growing crowd of people, who were trying to see who was in the shiny Ferrari, blasting music. "They know better! Calm down! We here to have some fun!"

After he finished rolling the joint, he got out of the car and lounged around for a minute. Kicking it with his men, as civilians stood around taking pictures and recording with their phones. Some were dancing and some were even bold enough to walk up to ask for pictures, but Donny didn't give his men permission to let them get too close. He had something better in store for them.

When he finished smoking the joint, he was feeling it, and one of his favorite songs from Manny just so happened to come up on his playlist. In the spur of the moment, Donny hopped on the hood of his Ferrari and began to dance along with the fans in the growing crowd, who were looking up at him in awe.

About halfway through the song, Donny felt that it was time to bring out his big surprise. There were about fifty people in the crowd, and it was steadily growing. People were literally pulling up to see him turn up, and he was about to give them something to turn up about.

He jumped off the car, popped the trunk, and called Marley and Jay over. There were about two-hundred thousand dollars in twenties sitting in the trunk. "Y'all help me throw this shit! Stand on top of y'all trucks though! We gon' make it rain on a sunny day!" he instructed enthusiastically before grabbing an arm full of bundles, placing them on his roof, and climbing back onto the top of his car.

He waited for Jay and Marley to do the same, and then it was on! They started throwing money into the air, and the crowd literally went crazy. People literally started running out of the mall to get their piece of the money. Even some employees from the food court abandoned their stations to join in the fun.

After Donny was finished throwing all the money, he smiled down at them scrambling to pick up the money. Kids had hands full of money, and he saw nothing but smiles on their faces. It made him feel good inside. Real good.

***

"Your boy is playing dangerous games out here," Ronte informed as he walked into the booth where Manny was recording a new mixtape.

Manny took his headphones off and looked at Ronte sideways. "I'm lost."

"Let me find you then." Ronte handed his phone to Manny.

Manny looked at the video of, Donny, throwing money onto civilians in the parking lot of the mall, with a growing smile on his face.

The caption under the video read, *"DG Donny blesses his community with $400,000 in cash."* The video had over six hundred thousand views already, and it was just uploaded a few hours ago.

"Oh, you think that shit funny, huh?" Ronte asked while snatching his phone out of Manny's hands.

"What's wrong with that? My nigga just giving back to his community. More niggas need to learn how to do that. He don't do strip clubs like that, so instead of throwing money on hoes, he threw it on his community. Shit, he needs a medal if you ask me," Manny retorted before shrugging his shoulders.

"What's wrong is that he's still in the game, shawty! He doing *too much* dirt in them streets to be drawing unwanted attention to himself like that. I fuck with you, and because of you, I fuck with him. I would hate to see that nigga end up a victim to the system. You need to talk to him because them crackers with the alphabets on their clothes will lock his ass up and melt the muthafuckin' key. If John Gotti ain't get away with it, he ain't gon' get away with it. He's bound to slip sooner or later."

Manny shrugged his shoulders again. "My nigga is out there living life, and he got his own mind. He gon' do what he do, all I tell him is to be smart about it. He knows the chances he's taking out there. He built for whatever comes with it. Good or bad."

"Okay," Ronte responded, with both hands up in surrender. "I'm gon' leave it at that... Go ahead and finish yo' verse so I can smash the rest of this song."

Manny shot him a mug. "You got me fucked up! I'm about to shine on yo ass for this song. I'm getting better by the day."

"Yeah, I can't argue with that, but not better than me. You got a long way to go, lil' nigga," Ronte boasted seriously before leaving Manny to it, but Donny was still on his mind.

Malik D. Rice

Chapter 6

Trappa bought a house across the street from Ridge Park upon his return. Everybody had counted him out and was shocked to see him back in the game with his old stripes back. That never happened. Once you were exiled in Dilluminati, you were always shamed, but Trappa was one of the lucky ones. At least that's what the streets were saying.

It was safe to say that shit wasn't the same as it was before he left. Everything had changed and it took some adjusting for Trappa, but he got it together after a while. What he couldn't get used to was the fact that his baby mother chose her life in Illinois over him. She chose to stay out there and raise their son in Illinois. He couldn't even be mad at her because they were better off without him, but it still hurt, and he didn't think he could ever heal from that. They were his life. It was kind of killing him slowly.

"Then the fucked-up part about all of it is that I don't even blame her for choosing a new life. This street shit ain't nothing but a means to an end, bruh. I be trying so hard to come to terms with the shit, but it ain't even that easy." He sat on his front porch, chopping it up with Rod. They'd always been close and became even closer since he'd been back in the game.

"That shit crazy. I can only imagine how I would feel if my wife pulled some shit like that," Rod said while pouring his second cup of VSOP into a plastic cup.

Trappa extended his arm so Rod could pour more liquor into his cup as well. "Then, on top of all that, I was on the phone with my son the other day and this lil' nigga kept bringing up Brian. So, I'm like who is Brian? I'm thinking it's his friend, but it turns out that it's Tia's *friend*. My muthafuckin' heart dropped, bruh. I ain't been gone a whole four months, and she already got niggas around my son."

"Noooooo!" Rod shouted loudly with wide eyes. "I know Tia ain't playin' like that! You pulled up on her about that shit yet?"

Trappa shook his head. "I was so hurt at the time, I just rushed him off the phone and smoked myself to sleep. That was two days ago and I ain't called back since... I curse Rondo *every day* for ripping me apart from everything I love."

Rod let out a low whistle. "That's cold right there... Guess what though? Believe it or not, Rondo was gon' let you slide since you left the city. You weren't in his way or making no noise. With all that shit he had going on; he had basically forgotten about you. You was good, but that nigga, Donny, told him that he needed you out here to move his work. Everybody knows you got a gift with making that work disappear," Rod informed with a straight face, even though he was lying through his teeth.

The shocking look that Trappa gave him let him know that he'd bitten the bait. The lie was believable, and he knew Trappa wouldn't confront Donny about the situation, so the seed was planted.

He didn't have an exact plan, but he did plan on turning as many people against Donny as he possibly could in hopes that it would help his agenda in some kind of way.

***

Gucci stepped out of her car and straightened herself out. She was about to knock Donny out of his socks with the new black Versace mini dress she wore. She'd just gotten her hair done the day before and the Versace heels she sported were fresh out of the box. Plus, she was smelling good. He wouldn't be able to resist her.

She strutted up the walkway and rang the doorbell, hoping he would answer, even though she knew better.

Marley came to the door and looked at her up and down with a lick of his lips. "Damn. You lookin' like a golden pork chop, girl."

"Where's my man?" she asked with a roll of her eyes. "I called and texted before I got here, but he didn't answer or respond."

Marley made a weird face. "He's upstairs, but he's busy right now."

"Busy? Let me in this house, Marley. He got me fucked up." She was furious.

"You know I can't do that right there. I'm just a small fry. You gon' have to take that up with him," he said before tightening his grip on the door just in case she left him no choice but to slam it in her face.

Gucci swallowed the lump in her throat and nodded her head understandably. "Okay, cool."

She walked off back to her car, got inside, and started blowing the horn like a woman who was being attacked. Just as she predicted, Donny came storming out of the house. Marley and Jay were behind him but kept their distance. They knew Donny could handle Gucci by himself.

She proceeded to get out of the car with a big smile on her face. "Hey, babyyyy!"

Donny didn't have a smile on his face though. He walked straight up to her and grabbed her by the throat roughly. "Bitch, what the fuck wrong with you? I know you know that you know better than this shit right here. You in *major* violation right now, hoe!" he spat before releasing her abruptly.

"Fuck you!" she spat with a hand on her neck. "You ignoring and dismissing me like I'm some regular bitch. That's what the fuck is wrong with me, nigga!"

Donny slapped his face and shook his head out of frustration. "Shawty. We had some good times once upon a time, but it ended at that. You my Mafioso, not my bitch. You don't got no room to be pulling up out here like this. Now, if you pull a move like this again, I'm gon' have to violate yo' ass. We getting too much money, so you need to get out yo' feelings. Our personal relationship is over with," he informed sternly before walking off without another word or glance.

Gucci was beyond pissed by Donny's stern dismissal of them. She was embarrassed and at a loss for words, so she stomped to the driver's side of her car, hopped in, and sped off with tears in her eyes.

Gucci swerved to a stop, in front of her mother's house. They really didn't talk much, since Ms. Dayna didn't believe in telephones, and Gucci didn't come by much, but she needed her mother right now, so she was there now.

She snatched the keys out of the car, took her heels off, and ran across the lawn into her mother's house.

"Maaa!" she yelled after letting herself in.

She went room to room looking for her but found her in her bed sound asleep. "Ma!"

"What, girl?" Ms. Dayna asked irritated. She didn't like to be awakened from her sleep, and Gucci was well aware of the fact.

"Why you clear the root-room out? Where's Donny's poppet? What happened?" Gucci asked hysterically, standing at the doorway, looking like a madwoman.

Ms. Dayna was awake now and she took her time sitting up in her bed before responding. "Gucci, I told you that man was powerful. I had no choice, but to undo all that was done on him. His ancestors began to haunt my dreams. It was only a matter of time before they began to haunt you, so I cut it short. I told you he was protected. Leave that man alone, Gucci."

"What!" Gucci shouted with wide eyes. "What about our ancestors?"

"His ancestors had to go through them to get to me, so obviously they're stronger. We had no business intervening on his soul anyway, Gucci. We were in the wrong. I'm strongly advising you to leave that man alone." Ms. Dayna had a little bass in her voice and her decision was final.

"Ughhhh! Fuck it, don't worry about it!" Gucci spat before storming off furiously.

Chapter 7

"That nigga damn near took over the whole north side, right up under my nose. Them disloyal ass niggas are all on this man's dick because he from the Motherland. Then he got the nerve to come to me talking about *kiss the ring*, and he'll let me keep my life. Shit is crazy," Cleezy vented to Donny, who sat across from him at a restaurant table. They met up at Outback on the west side.

Donny looked at him emotionlessly. "To be honest, I really don't give a fuck about your life, Cleezy. The only reason why I need you alive is because I know what type of damage a nigga like Falcon can do with your type of power."

"Fuck you, lil' nigga. I don't need yo' help. I never even asked you to intervene, that was your decision," Cleezy spat.

"Yes, you do need me. That's your pride talking right there. I did my homework and that nigga, Falcon, ain't nothing to be played with. He's one of them smooth killers that turn other niggas into killers. You, on the other hand, turn niggas into hustlers. Who you think gon' win that war between y'all?" Donny retorted matter-a-factly.

Donny's cockiness and nonchalance were getting up under Cleezy's skin, as usual. He slumped back in his seat a little and contemplated Donny's words. As much as he *really* hated to admit it, Donny was right. Dilluminati's aid was exactly what he needed to come out on top. Once again, he found himself putting his pride to the side in the presence of this young man. "Aight, man. You got a plan?"

"Of course. Fight fire with fire, but on your turf because mine is too hot. When my guys ride, they gon' wear blue bandannas, so Falcon thinks it's your men. It'll give us an advantage if he doesn't know that DG is involved right now. Plus, it makes you look stronger. He'll think that he underestimated you... Oh yeah, this shit gon' run you $400,000. It should be more, but I'm feeling generous today."

***

Tirasia made about a hundred thousand when she moved to Atlanta for a year. She stripped at the infamous club called *Strokers* and lived below her means, so she could stack her money and get out of the game. When she reached her quota, she packed her things and moved back to her hometown. It wasn't much, compared to Atlanta, but it was home and she felt at ease there.

She invested her money into a large beauty supply store and has been on cruise control since then. She felt successful by being a twenty-year-old entrepreneur. Now, she was on a mission to find love. That was next on her list of goals. She'd failed poorly a few times over the past year, but she really felt like she had something in Antonio.

He didn't wear his heart on his sleeve, but she *knew* he had deep feelings for her. He had plenty of extravagant women begging him for attention, but he chose to give it to her. That had to count for something.

She really didn't want to deal with the whole Falcon situation, but she knew that it was important to Antonio, so she had to find a way to make it happen. She was a well-respected Crip Queen in the city, and her name held some weight now that she made something of herself. She would use that to get in good with Falcon.

The security bell connected to the front door of her store going off broke her train of thought. Her home girl, Jazzy, came strolling into the store, looking ghetto fabulous as usual. "What's up, bitch? You must got a free weave giveaway going on or some shit? The way you rushed me down here!"

Tirasia stood up from her seat behind the counter with a mug plastered on her face. "Girl, calm yo' ratchet ass down! I got customers up in here," she spat in an undertone before walking around the counter, so she could lead Jazzy to her office in the back.

"What's yo' problem? You acting real weird today," Jazzy asked after they were in the office.

Tirasia stood in front of her. "Listen. I got a lil' job for you, but I need you on point, Jazzy. This is serious business right here."

"As long as I don't have to suck no wrinkled dick, I'm with it," Jazzy responded seriously.

Tirasia chuckled and shook her head. "Shit, it shouldn't be wrinkled, but I'm gon' pay you a few thousand. You can buy a lot of weave with that. Plus, you can keep whatever you milk the nigga out of."

Malik D. Rice

Chapter 8

Gino and Danger were at odds. Danger paced the floor in front of Gino trying to talk some sense into his son's thick head. "I do understand where you coming from. You think I wasn't young and dumb like you before lil' nigga? You're supposed to be a young boss. Young bosses don't go on missions with the shooters, that defeats the whole purpose. They sit back and plot their next move while the soldiers out making those moves."

Danger's wisdom went into one of Gino's ears and exited out of the other. "My men love me the way they do because I don't tell them to do shit that I wouldn't do myself."

"How many times you got to show them? You ain't got to do everything yourself. They should know by now that you gon' get down and dirty. You a bad muthafucka, but don't be stupid, son. You not gon' last like that," said Danger with plenty of aggravation.

"You said you were with me, right? Be with me. If you not with me, you against me."

Danger shook his head disappointedly. There was no way he was going to let Gino go on the mission by himself. "You gon' be the death of me... Let's go, man!"

***

Falcon was in one of his many trap spots overseeing a major drug deal that was about to go down shortly. He was in his own zone, listening to DG Rell's new mixtape.

"How you planning on going to war with these niggas, and all you listen to is they music?" X asked curiously. He was Falcon's head of security and close friend. He went everywhere Falcon went.

Falcon gave him a blank look. "So, I don't got nothing against them. This shit just business. Plus, DG Rell be talking about some real shit."

"Whatever. They alright, but I think they're overrated. Fuck 'em."

"You just a Super Crip, fool! You don't like nobody that ain't throwing up a C," Falcon joked seriously.

X shrugged unapologetically. "Why should I? If it ain't blue, it ain't true."

Falcon was laughing at his friend when one of his lieutenants rushed into the dining room. "Some niggas just rolled through one of our blocks and did five of the baby gangsters dirty!" His voice was very urgent.

"Who? Where?" X asked after jumping up out of his seat.

"Over by them new apartment buildings on Troy Boulevard."

Falcon stood up out of his chair. "Oh, hell nah! I got to see this." He stormed off towards the front door.

"The plug is on the way right now," X reminded, stopping Falcon short.

"We'll be back in time. I just want to see the damage. Come on. Leave two of the soldiers here just in case the plug beat us back."

By the time Falcon made it to the crime scene, there were blue lights, yellow tape, and news vans everywhere. X parked the blue BMW truck and they hopped out for a closer look at the carnage.

They spotted a group of soldiers from the hood standing together in a distance and made their way over there.

"What the fuck happened out here, man?" X asked with his booming voice. He was already a big, black, gorilla-looking ass nigga, so his aggressive persona made most people feel uneasy around him. The group of young gangsters in front of them were no exception.

"Two trucks pulled up on the corner and did them niggas the foul way. Real overkill type shit. It was so many shots going off, it sounded like non-stop thunder. A few of the lil' shorties that were in the playground across the street saw the shit and was confused because the niggas that hopped out shooting had on blue flags," the squad leader informed with a heavy heart. He was close to all five of the victims.

X turned around and looked at Falcon. "I ain't know Cleezy had it in him."

"They just dropped two more homies on the other side of the boulevard," one of the soldiers informed from the crowd. He was still on his phone receiving the news. "Same shit. Niggas had on blue rags."

Falcon punched his open left hand, with his right fist. "Fuck!"

***

Cleezy lounged in his man-cave with Blu, watching the news. They were stunned by what they saw. "Damn! Them DG niggas ain't playing. What got into them niggas? They ain't been like that," Blu asked.

"They trying to live up to the image Manny painting of them," Cleezy hypothesized.

Blu shook his head rapidly. "They ain't trying to do shit. They already doing it. We might have to get one of the lil' homies to drop a mixtape to give these lazy ass niggas some motivation," he joked seriously.

"Yeah, I know right." Cleezy chuckled. "We got to start violating niggas. Setting consequences for slackers. If a nigga ain't bringing something to the table, he gon' get treated like *nothing*."

Blu nodded his agreement. "Yeah. We've been spoiling these niggas. It's time to bring that iron fist out, huh?"

"Fuckin' right! All that lollygagging ain't gon' cut it. We've got to establish another structure quickly! They not gon' want to end up like them seven dead homies on the news."

Blu stood up from the couch they sat on. "Fuck that! I got you big homie. I'm about to gather up the OG's, and we gon' handle this shit now."

Malik D. Rice

Chapter 9

Persia was sitting back in the comfortable soft leather chair with her eyes closed while an Asian woman tended to her feet. She felt so calm and relaxed until she heard a familiar voice. "If my lil' Demons saw me in a nail salon getting my feet done, they'll try to kill me their damn selves," Dizzy joked while sitting in the chair next to hers. Another Asian woman was setting up her supplies to tend to his feet.

Persia opened her eyes, took off her Versace shades, and looked at him shockingly. "What the hell are you doing here? How'd you find me?"

"You had your location on when you posted that picture on Instagram," he informed truthfully.

"I'll never do that again... What do you want, Dizzy?"

He gave her a knowing look. "I already told you in the Walgreens. I want yo' ass. Plain and simple."

"If you haven't noticed, I'm happily taken," she retorted matter-a-factly.

"Yeah, I kind of went for that shit until I saw that you liked most of my pictures on Instagram. That was after we ran into each other in Walgreen's. You can't be *happily taken* if you went and found my page after that. You must like what you see."

Persia rolled her pretty little eyes. "It was innocent, Dizzy. Do you stalk every girl that likes your picture on Instagram?"

"You know better than that. I could give a fuck about a bitch, but it's something about yo' lil' ass," he stated, looking her up and down while licking his lips. "I tell you what. Just let me lick it."

Persia gave him a wide-eyed look, like a little schoolgirl.

Fifteen minutes later, they were at Persia's house in her bedroom. Persia laid back on her bed, with her skirt pulled up, while Dizzy was on his knees, slurping up her juices and sucking on her clit, like a fucking pornstar.

"Ooooowwwww! Sssssss!" She gripped a handful of his thick dreads. "Boy, don't do me like that!" she ranted with her eyes rolling behind her head. She didn't think she ever had her pussy ate like that before.

He took two fingers and started plunging them into her rapidly, while he continued to work his tongue on her clit. He knew what he was doing, and he kept doing it.

All of a sudden, he removed his face from between her legs and looked up at her. "Turn around."

"Huh?" she asked, even though she heard him clearly. That head he just gave her left her tingly and dumb.

He knew what she was going through, so he hooked his arm between her legs and flipped her over roughly.

"Oh!" She was very turned on by him and his aggressiveness.

Dizzy got back on his knees, put his face back between her legs, and went back to work on her pussy. He put two fingers back in her pussy and one in her ass. She felt her climax rising instantly. "God damn, boy! Ssshit!"

After she came twice, Dizzy stood up and looked down at her grimly with a long hard dick pointing right at her.

"I don't know why you looking at me like that. The party's over. You did your job, and I got my rocks off," she teased seductively, but she wasn't looking at him. She had all eyes on that dick.

A slow smile formed on Dizzy's face and nodded his head up and down. "Aight, cool." He turned around and started to put on his clothes.

"Oh, so now you just gon' give up that easily?" Persia asked disappointedly. "I thought you were a taker? You better come take this pussy, boy!"

Dizzy stopped dressing instantly. His back was turned to her as he flashed a bright smile quickly before turning around towards her with his game face on. He was about to nail her little ass to the cross.

***

"Woahhh! That's a big step right there, bro. It's only been a few months. You thinking about marriage already?" Sasha asked Tadoe.

He sat on Sasha's kitchen counter, looking down at her amused. "Nah, this ring ain't for that. It's just something to solidify our bond."

"Damn. I can't remember you taking anybody this seriously. You really think she the one?" Sasha asked curiously.

Tadoe shrugged. "I don't know. She's good enough for a nigga to settle down with. I know she got a past and she ain't perfect, but neither am I, so fuck it. Got to take a chance on somebody. I'm not getting any younger."

Sasha nodded. "Yeah, you're right. That's my girl and all, but I knew you longer. I hope she don't hurt you."

Tadoe shrugged his shoulders again. "You saw all the women that I hurt in my time. If she does me dirty, I'll just chalk the shit up to karma. Karma's like the government, you got to pay them taxes."

"Bruh, are you never not nonchalant? You don't care about shit."

"I care about certain things and people. I just make it a point to try and understand life, and the people in it, as much as possible."

Sasha turned the stove off and threw the cleaning rag on the counter. "You're right, but she's a good girl. A little young for you, but I feel she has your best interest at heart."

Chapter 10

Jay woke Donny up out of his sleep. "Bruh, get the fuck up!" He shook Donny abruptly.

"What? What?" Donny spat as he jumped out of the bed alertly, and hurriedly grabbed his mini-AK-74 from the nightstand. He was about to storm out of the room, but Jay stopped him short.

"Where the hell are you going?"

"I don't know, nigga! It better be something going on with the way you just woke me up out of my sleep. Who died?"

Jay shook his head. "Nobody nigga. I ain't wake you up for that, and even if I did, you weren't about to go out there and do shit. You the head of the city, nigga, wake yo' ass up. I got some news for you."

Donny took a deep breath and calmed himself down. He was psyched out, in savage mode, but he had to remember who he was, and where he was in life. "You right. I tripped out... Wassup though? What happened bruh?" He tossed the gun on his bed and took a seat, looking up at Jay patiently.

"Look like you done pushed Gucci to the limit. That bitch done finally snapped."

Donny's eyes grew wide. "What she do? Killed herself?"

"Nah, but she might want to when you get finished with her ass," Jay admitted. "Turn yo' phone on and you gon' see what I'm talking about."

Donny's phone was on, but he put it on airplane mode last night so that he could get a full night's sleep. He grabbed his phone and took it off of airplane mode. It hadn't buzzed like that since he got out of jail a few months ago.

DG Donny's new sex tape! That's what the news alert read across his screen as it popped up.

He went to the video and couldn't believe his eyes. Gucci really leaked their personal sex tape. He really had forgotten all about that. He slipped up and let her convince him to let her record them one day. "I'm gon' kill that bitch!" he spat, before throwing his phone to the wall, breaking it upon impact.

***

Gucci was at the Pretty Girl's Mansion, throwing a full fit. "Which one of y'all hoes did it? Because I don't let nobody else close enough to gain access to my phone and leak that video!"

"Gucci, we would never..." one of her girls started to say, but was cut off before she could finish.

"Bitch, shut the fuck up!" Gucci barked with her purple Glock pointed at the girl's head. "I didn't leak the video, so that means one of y'all hoes did. Now, which one of y'all hating ass bitches did it?" She was boarder line hysterical. She had to get to the bottom of it before Donny got to her ass.

"You not gon' get no results like this, Gucci. You need to chill out," Zip advised gently, trying to calm her friend down. She felt the situation beginning to spiral out of control.

"Chill out! That nigga, Donny, probably on the way over here to whack me right now and you got the nerve to tell me to chill out. Fuck that! I need some answers *right now*!"

Boc!

She let loose a warning shot, into the floor, just inches away from the couch where four of her girls were sitting.

"Woaahhh! Gucci, you got to calm the fuck down! You gon' end up doing something you regret!" Zip stood up from another couch with both hands up, walking towards her old friend.

Gucci turned her pistol onto Zip. "Zip, I love you like a blood sister, but if you take another step, you not gon' leave me no choice."

"What? You gon' shoot *me*? After all the shit we done been through. Nah, that's not even you. Put the fuckin' gun down and we gon' go get to the bottom of this shit, the right way."

Boc!

Gucci squeezed off a shot, but Zip was still walking forward, so she squeezed the trigger a second time. *Boc!*

Screams came from her girls, as some of them fled for safety and others rushed to the floor, trying to save Zip, who was now hanging onto her life.

"Look what you did! What's wrong with you?" one of her girls shouted while applying pressure to Zip's chest where the bullets had struck.

It was then that Gucci had finally realized what she'd just done. It's like she'd been snapped out of a trance. "Shit! Shit!" Tears escaped her eyes as she peered down at her best friend. "What the hell did I just do?" she asked, barely above a whisper. Nobody heard her, but her. Just like nobody knew she didn't mean to do it, but her. Shit was ugly before, but it was hideous now.

She dropped her gun on the floor and went to go grab her phone so that she could call for help. "Hang on, Zip! Help is on the way! They coming! Hang on, baby girl! I'm so sorry!" she informed after getting off the phone while applying pressure to Zip's wounds.

After witnessing the damage, Donny got dressed and headed out. He had Marley drive him straight to Gucci's house because he had no patience to wait on his driver, but she wasn't there, so they went to the Pretty Girl Mansion, but obviously, they were too late.

It was a circus in the front yard. Police cruisers and ambulance trucks surrounded the house with crime scene tape and a group of spectators. They were just in time to watch Gucci be escorted from her house into a police cruiser by two officers.

"What the fuck going on out here?" Donny asked, even though he knew Marley or Jay didn't know the answer to that question.

"Hold on, let me go find out," Marley said, before unfastening his seatbelt, and hopping out of the car.

Two short minutes later, Marley, hopped back into the car. "That bitch done shot Zip. She ain't dead, but the word on the street is that she ain't in good condition though."

"Damn... I don't know if her lucky day is today, or her luck has run out completely," Donny stated honestly.

Jay turned around in his seat and looked dead at Donny with a very serious expression. "Nigga, Gucci is your money handler. It might be your unlucky day."

Chapter 11

Gucci sat at the cold metal table in the interrogation room with her head in between her arms. She couldn't stop crying. She wasn't sobbing, but the tears wouldn't stop. She was fucked all the way around the board. Her head was spinning, and she couldn't even think straight.

She'd been sitting in that room for, what felt like, hours. She was cold, hungry, and tired. She just wanted to go to sleep and wake up from this nightmare, but she knew it was her reality. A harsh reality that would change her life forever. It was hitting her harder and harder, the longer she sat in that room.

"Ahhhhhhhhh!" She yawned loudly while sitting up in her chair and stretching her arms in the same motion.

She wiped the tears from her eyes with the back of her hand and looked around the small room. Her eyes settled on the reflective mirror and they stayed there. She could feel the eyes behind the glass, looking at her. Studying her like a lab rat.

The door to the room opened and a middle-aged Caucasian man with a big head walked in playing music from a phone. It was one of Manny's hottest songs, and to her surprise, he started dancing along to the beat. What surprised her ever more, is that he actually had some rhythm. He had to have some black friends or family.

When he was finished putting on his show, he cut the music off and took a seat across from her. He wasn't dressed in a suit like they were on the TV shows. He was actually fresh as hell in a pair of True Religion jeans and Jordan's. "If it ain't Ms. DG Gucci. You look better in your pictures, but I'll just chalk that up to all the crying you've been doing."

Gucci didn't say a word, just stuck up her middle finger, giving a silent *fuck you.*

"I mean that would be nice. I must admit, I watched the sex tape, and I'd be lying if I said I didn't run to the bathroom to jack off to it. You could've had a *bright* future in the porn business, young lady."

Gucci wasn't expecting the interrogation to go like this. The man was being rude and offensive. It was starting to get under her skin, but she tried her best to hold it together. "I have a lawyer, and I want her present."

"Yeah, I hear you, but fuck all that for right now. This conversation isn't on the record. I'm not here about your friend. I don't care why you shot her, but I'm not going to lie, I'm glad you did. You just made this a lot easier for us."

***

"You need to get out of town. I can't see Gucci holding all that water. They just reported that Zip died in the hospital last night. That aggravated assault just got boosted up to a murder charge. You think Gucci is that solid?" Jay asked, already knowing the answer.

Donny took a deep breath. He hadn't said too much since yesterday. He'd been in deep thought, trying to figure shit out. "I'm not leaving my post. They gon' have to drag me out this muthafucka," he informed stubbornly.

"I got orders from Rondo to stay out here in Rondoville, but I don't have to stay in this house. It's too risky for me since I'm already on the run. I'm gon' find me a decent lil' low-key spot, around the way. I'm gon' be in the shadows, but I'm always gon' be one call away if you need me to handle *anything*." Jay informed genuinely.

"You lame as fuck. Soon as shit get a lil' ruff, you gon' run like a lil' bitch." Marley spat, after hopping in Jay's face.

Jay returned eye contact with him. "Marley, if you don't get out my face, I'm gon' knock yo' big ass out! And that's on the 4's!"

"Ain't nobody gon' do shit!" Donny barked in an irritated tone. "Y'all niggas calm the fuck down... Jay, that's a good idea. I'm not mad at you for it." He looked at, Marley. "And you need pack yo' shit too because you about to join the rest of yo' brothers on the road with Manny."

Marley shook his head from side to side rapidly. "Hell nah, bruh! I'm staying here with you."

"That's an order, Marley. Go pack yo' shit!" Donny commanded firmly, before walking off, upstairs to his bedroom.

***

Later on that night, Tadoe showed up on Donny's doorstep. When Donny answered the front door himself, he was mildly shocked. "Where yo' guard dogs at?"

"Gone," Donny answered flatly, before walking back into the house with the door wide open.

Tadoe walked inside and closed the door behind himself. "What's going on lil' bruh? It's just a sex tape, it happens to the best of us. You're technically a celebrity, so it was only a matter of time anyway."

"It's deeper than that, but I'm glad you came over here though because we need to talk. I know how you like to distance yourself away from the real street shit, but I'm gon' need you to step up. You and Dizzy gon' be running the camp. Y'all got to keep shit above water. The structure got to remain in place because if Rondo got to come out of hiding, it's not gon' be good for *nobody*," Donny warned while pouring himself a bowl of cereal at the table in the kitchen.

Tadoe was still standing, glaring down at Donny, looking highly confused. "What the fuck going on, Donny? You talking like you going somewhere."

"I am, nigga. It might not be today, and it might not be tomorrow, but one of these days, Gucci gon' tell what she knows and I'm gon' be gon' for a while. Y'all niggas got to hold this shit down and keep shit airtight out here."

Tadoe sat down, openmouthed. "Damn! I ain't even think about it like that. You really think she gon' tell?"

Donny dropped his fork and gave Tadoe a knowing look.

Malik D. Rice

.

Chapter 12

It's been a long and lonely ten days since Gucci got hauled away in hand-cuffs. Right when Donny started giving her the benefit of doubt and starting to think that she'd maybe kept it solid for a change, he heard his name being called on a bullhorn, waking him up out of his sleep.

"Donald Redfarn, come outside with your hands locked behind your head! We have this whole area surrounded! We are prepared to breach the property and use excessive force if needed!"

Surprisingly, Donny wasn't even tripping. After all, he was expecting them anyway. He'd been preparing for this day for nine days now. He had his digital money moved numerous times, until it reached its final destination in private numbered accounts overseas. He had most of his cash and jewelry stuffed inside of a safe that was buried deep in the woods. He only had necessities in the house.

He got up, changed into three pairs of white boxers, and got dressed. He took a few pulls from a blunt of weed and did a gram of molly before walking downstairs.

He walked outside fresh as hell, draped in designer threads and the YF chain Manny gave him. He had a smug smirk on his face for the news cameras. If the world had to see him being dragged away, he would do it with his head held high and a smile on his face just like Dinero did when they hauled him away.

A group of heavily armed agents came and cuffed him up, after patting him down. After whispering a few insulting remarks at him and reading him his Miranda rights, they escorted him to one of the vehicles.

"Donny! Donny! The authorities have revealed that they have some serious charges against you! Do you have anything to say to all of your admirers out there that are watching this right now?" a female reporter asked eagerly as he passed by.

Donny looked straight at the camera and yelled, "Dlatttt! My Loyalty 4Eva! Ain't nothin' else to be said, man." He walked away, but his nonchalant energy remained. It was a short interview that was sure to make the headlines and history.

***

"I'm about to bump that lil' nigga all the way up to a Capo! That was some *gangsta ass shit* right there! He went out with a bigger bang than me, baby!" Dinero admitted excitedly.

Ladie shook her head sadly. "That's a damn shame. That lil' boy had so much potential, but he was in way over his head. That much money and power ain't meant for everybody."

"Yeah," Dinero agreed, even though he knew better.

Donny was obviously built to be a boss, but the government had to make an example out of him, and there was nothing Dinero could do about that. It wasn't even about him being big in the game. He was just too famous, and a famous kingpin was destined for failure.

Dinero knew this because he was once in Donny's shoes. He got locked up because Rell was screaming his name, just like Manny screamed Donny's name. Donny had to take one for the team, just like he did. At the end of the day, it was just business.

***

Manny was on stage in London, doing a show when Venom muscled his way to the front of the stage and showed Manny the video of Donny being escorted with handcuffs on. The caption read, *"Notorious kingpin captured, but has no regret"*.

"Hold the fuck up! Stop the muthafuckin' music!" Manny commanded sternly.

The DJ instantly stopped the music and the club quieted down, trying to see what was wrong with Manny. "Aye, DJ play this shit on the big screen. I wanna hear this shit," he instructed seriously before removing his shirt. His temperature had just risen tremendously.

Venom gave Von the phone and Von gave it to the DJ. The DJ got the phone, hooked it up to the big screen behind the stage, and played the twenty-second video clip for the whole club to see and hear.

After seeing the video, Manny wiped the tears that had escaped from his eyes. He still had his back facing the crowd.

Payback walked up to him, facing the crowd. "We can cancel this show if you want to lil' bruh. Yo' fans will understand."

"Nah, I'm gon' do it for Donny," Manny assured, before lifting the mic up to his lips. "Aye, DJ... Listen! Give me a beat! Not one of my beats though, just any beat, but make sure that muthafucka hard. You should know how I'm feeling inside right now. Drop some shit, so I can make them feel it too."

It took about twenty long seconds, but the DJ found the right beat and dropped that muthafucka. It came on with a soft guitar and piano keys playing. It brought instant tears back to Manny's eyes, but it didn't matter. He had to vent and release his pain, or he would explode. Rapping was his therapy, and he was about to give it to them raw. A freestyle straight from his soul.

He turned around when the beat dropped and let it rip!

Have you ever lost somebody to the dope gameee?
Try to tell them youngin's,
take it slow, maneeee!
Think you doing good,
but cause more painnnn!
I lost my brother,
to the dope gameeee!

I never thought they'd catch my dawg,
but this shit real!
Always thought my problems ended,
with a record deal!
How I feel?
Shit, I'm feeling like a burning house!
Remember, Donny pulled a nigga out a burning house!

The crowd rocked with him and flowed with the vibe as hundreds of shining lights shined from recording phones. They felt Manny's pain and made sure to let him know that he had plenty of support.

Manny felt their energy as he continued to pour his soul out onto the beat. He felt their energy, and they pumped him up to go harder. His eyes were still watery, and he could barely see the crowd, but he kept going.

He rode the beat all the way out to the end and dropped the mic before exiting the stage. Everyone understood, and no one offered any protest. He gave them a show to remember.

Chapter 13

Gino cruised around the city solo in his truck thinking about his next move. Donny's demise changed the game. He didn't know who was going to take Donny's spot, and that didn't sit well with him.

He pulled up to a large hidden park right outside of the city that was home to a mixture of trailers and RV's of different sizes. He'd ridden past the park a thousand times, but never really paid any attention to it, until now.

It was low-key, and the trees were a good cover to give the tenants some privacy between their spots. Gino pulled up to the only RV with four American flags hanging from each end.

Jay sat on the steps, smoking a cigarette. He didn't have on any jewelry or designer clothing. He wore black Adidas jogging pants, a white tank top, and a pair of black and white Adidas slippers.

Gino parked and hopped out. "You alright, my nigga?" he asked while looking at Jay suspiciously. "You out here in the boondocks on some weird shit. I can't remember the last time I saw you without a neck full of jewelry. Where the hell yo trophies at, bruh?" He grabbed one of his chains for emphasis.

"When I split up with Donny and went solo, I tucked everything away in a safe spot. I only kept forty thousand to live off of. I'm on some low-key shit these days, so that should last me for a long lil' minute. I'm on the run, so I don't need to be drawing no attention," Jay informed wisely. He'd been having long talks with Rondo lately.

Gino nodded his understanding. "Yeah, I keep forgetting you on the run... Anyway, you heard anything from Rondo? I'm trying to figure out who gon' take Donny's spot."

"Nequa."

Gino raked his brain, rushing to put a face with the name. "You talking about Nequa who left? She back in town?"

"Not yet, but the word is already sent out. She'll be back any day now."

Gino sighed while shaking his head side-to-side. "You think she can handle all this shit?"

"Shit, I don't know," Jay shrugged his shoulders nonchalantly. "I don't know her too well, but she was chosen for a reason... I guess we'll see."

Gino took a deep breath before shaking Jay's hand again. "Yeah, I guess we will see. I'm gon' catch you later though, bruh. All this country-ass scenery is killing my vibe. I got to get up out of here."

"Stay on your toes out there, bro. I know you on your wild boy shit, but you need to pump your breaks," Jay warned, as Gino walked back towards his truck.

"They call it the fast life for a reason, my nigga," Gino retorted, before jumping into his truck and smashing off.

***

Nequa's plane landed at Fayetteville's airport, and although it felt good to be home, she wasn't too excited. She wanted to return on her own terms, but fate had dealt her a different hand.

After Manny took her spot all those months ago, she went to Rondo and requested a transfer to Detroit where she started an online gambling company with her male cousin. She was living comfortably out there and was enjoying her retirement until Tadoe gave her a call with the disturbing news.

She knew the curses that came with being a made man and she tried to reject the position, but apparently, *her camp needed her*. She was left with no choice. She rented a car and headed straight to Tadoe's house. Her family and friends would have to wait.

Nequa knocked on Tadoe's door firmly. She had a bone to pick with him, and it couldn't wait.

"One second!" a soft and polite female voice, said, from the other side of the door.

A couple of seconds later, a pretty little mixed girl with short hair, answered the door. She scanned Nequa up and down, but not challengingly. Just curiously. "Hey. You here for Tadoe?"

"Yeah. Tell him that Nequa's out here and needs to talk to him about some business."

"Come in. You don't have to wait out here. You can wait on him I'm in the living room," Persia said before ushering Nequa into the living room.

"He's sleep, but I'm about to wake him up. Hold on."

After Persia disappeared, Nequa began to look around the place and admire Tadoe's taste. He'd fixed the place up nicely. The inside was way more spacious than it looked from the outside.

A few minutes later, Tadoe walked down the stairs in nothing but a pair of Ralph Lauren pajama pants, while rubbing the cold from his eyes. "Nequa. It's nice to meet you, but why didn't you set up a meeting? That's how shit works at this level."

"With all due respect, Tadoe, I don't want this position. That's why I'm here right now. Out of all these Mafiosos out here, you couldn't have picked anybody else? Why me? Rondo gave me a pass to do my own thing up in Detroit," she asked curiously. She really wasn't up to deal with all the bullshit that she knew would come with her position.

Tadoe chuckled while staring at her with an amused expression. "You think I summoned you out here? Hell nah! I'm the Top Don, but this is over my head. Jay pulled up on me about a week ago and told me if anything happens to Donny, you will take his spot. Apparently, he's the only one with a direct line to Rondo, so that's the man you need to talk to. Until then, I suggest you get comfortable in that house down there. Donny already had everything he cares about moved out of the house."

Nequa raked her brain trying to put a face with the name Jay. "You talking about the skinny black kid that came up here with Rondo?"

"Yeah, they're real cousins."

"Where do I find him then?"

Tadoe shrugged. "Your guess is as good as mines, but he'll have to get you up to speed and fill you in on the new structure. So, I'm guessing he'll find you."

Malik D. Rice

Chapter 14

Jazzy laid on her stomach while X's big ass kneeled on top of her, pumping his life away. She moaned sexily for him, but it was all an act. He was too big for his dick to be that small. It had a little thickness to it, of course, but he didn't have any length to get in her guts, and that's what she needed to get off.

All three of her other boyfriends were working with a little something, so to go from that to this was depressing. If Tirasia wasn't paying her so much money, she wouldn't be putting up with this bullshit.

"There you go, daddy! I'm about to cum again!" she lied intensely. "I need you to cum with me! Concentrate on that nut, nigga!"

X loved the encouragement and started stroking faster. "Throw that ass back, bitch!" he commanded with two hard slaps on her ass.

"Yes! Keep slapping my ass! That's gon' make me cum!" she was telling the truth this time.

X obliged, and she lived up to her word by creaming all over his dick. He came shortly after and collapsed on the bed.

Jazzy took it upon herself to go get a warm rag to clean herself up, then she pulled the condom off of his penis that was shrinking even more and cleaned him up a little. After that, she got up and went to the bathroom, where she cleaned herself a little more.

When she walked back into the hotel bedroom, she stopped and put a hand on her hip. "You just gon' hit and run, huh?"

"A nigga like me can't lay up in bed all day. I'm on a mission, baby," said X while pulling the last leg in his Dickie pants.

"Anything I can do to help? All you got to do is ask around about me. I'm not gon' lie like I'm wifey material, but I am a down bitch, and I ride for the set for the right cause," she assured confidently.

X looked at her with a smirk while pulling his shirt over his belly. "Shit, that sounds like my kind of wifey material right there. Matter of fact, get dressed, you coming with me."

***

Blu slid Dizzy a book bag under the restaurant table. It was filled with large bills. "That's the money Cleezy was supposed to give Donny, but he's out the picture now, so we'll carry on our arrangement with you. Falcon is a threat to us both, so our unity is wise."

"Where the hell is Cleezy anyway?" Dizzy asked while peeping inside of the bag at its contents.

"I convinced him to get lost until things settled down while I handled things out here. No need for the king to be in the field," Blu informed truthfully. "We doing what we been doing, or you got plans of your own?"

"Ain't nothing wrong with Donny's plan. Just let me know the block you want sprayed up and we'll handle it, but don't abuse that. I know you got soldiers of your own, so I'm not gon' be overly sacrificing mines. Just hit me up when needed."

Blu nodded his understanding instantly. "Of course. I wouldn't have it any other way." He extended his hand out for a shake, and their bond was sealed.

***

Trappa took a trip over to Rod's domain to chill with his old friend. Rod had two trailers in his hood. One where he stayed with his wife and daughter, the other was only a two-bedroom where he used as a man cave. They lounged in the air-conditioned man cave, on the blazing summer day.

Although they were old friends, they were becoming extremely close, ever since Trappa came back from Illinois. "I'm not even gon' lie, I never been too fond of Nequa, but I rather her sitting on that throne than Donny," Rod admitted while laying back on the couch.

Trappa sat up in a comfy chair. "Nequa, that's my dawg. I'm glad she got the spot too. She definitely gon' do the right thing... You think Donny chose who was gon' take his spot or Rondo?"

"Probably Donny since he was in Nequa's camp before. I doubt it was Rondo, ain't nobody heard from the nigga in months. I hear he's on some *real* next-level type of shit," Rod informed.

"Yeah, makes sense... Let's watch *Pain In Full*. I need some motivation," Trappa instructed.

Rod happily obliged.

***

"This will be our last meeting. We're about to turn the investigation over to the police detectives who are just going to end up letting you guys buy the investigation anyway," Craig informed nonchalantly. He had set up a late-night meeting with Rod to break the news.

They were in the back of a closed barbershop on Murchison Road, leaning on the hoods of their cars that were parked facing each other. "Damn, so this whole investigation was really for Donny?"

"No. At first, we planned on gaining enough evidence to do a full sweep out here. But after a little while, our superiors let us know that they only wanted Donny, so we hacked Gucci's phone and leaked the sex tape. It was way more effective than we thought it would be."

Rod stood straight up with wide eyes. "Damnnnnn! That was y'all?" he asked, surprised that they played the game that dirty.

"Yeah, I was actually against the idea, but it wasn't an idea. It was an order, there wasn't too much I could do about it... Anyway, we're about to move our investigation to Tallahassee, Florida to cage another one of Dilluminati's rising stars," he informed bluntly.

Rod shook his head. Craig had just revealed a number of things to him with those last two statements. "Aight, Craig. I can't speak for your organization, but you ain't too bad yourself," he admitted before walking around to the driver's seat of his car.

"Rod!" Craig stopped him short before he got into the car. "It might not be this year or the next, but you owe us a favor and we won't forget. When we need you, you need to be ready to do your part. Don't leave this city."

"That's fair," said Rod before hopping in his car and pulling off slowly.

Malik D. Rice

Chapter 15

Jay was never a friendly person and didn't plan on changing that now, but there were few people that appealed to him and the lady he spotted doing yoga in between the trees was no different.

He was in the backyard of his RV, grilling chicken on his small grill for dinner. The sun was almost gone. He was curious as to why that fine ass lady was alone doing yoga in the dark, so he dropped the spatula and went to go ask her.

He took his Glock out of his front pocket and tucked it into his pants on his waist as he approached her.

"And who are you?" she asked in a sweet feminine voice.

"Just a basic young nigga... You got some good ears," he answered. Her head was facing the other way when he walked up, and he knew for a fact that he was light on his feet.

She took a couple of deep breaths before standing straight up and facing him. "Well, it's nice to meet you, Young Nigga. Plus, I do have good hearing. Most blind people do."

That took Jay by surprise. He'd never actually met a blind person before and never seen one as fine as her. Her skin was light, but her light grey eyes were even lighter. She was definitely blind. "Damn! I would've never known. Why you out here by yourself like this? And my name is Jay."

"I come out here three nights out of the week to do my yoga and meditate. I've been out here for years and everyone around here knows I don't like to be interrupted during, so I knew you had to be new around here... You probably had all type of game you wanted to spit to me before you found out I was blind, huh?"

Jay shook his head with a smirk. "Not really. I really thought you were the FEDs, to be honest. Shit looked kind of staged."

"Wow, I never heard that one before! Well, my name is Deanna and I obviously don't work with the FBI. But the fact that you're cautious of them surveilling you, says a lot about you."

"Can I walk you back to your RV? I would feel terrible if I didn't."

She noticed his swift change of conversation and respected it. There was no way for her to tell exactly how he looked, but his voice was low yet firm and he had some strong energy. She kind of felt him approaching before she'd actually heard him. "There's no need. Here come my sisters. They must've seen me talking a strange guy."

Jay looked up and seen two women jogging their way.

"Deannaaaa!" one of the women yelled out frantically.

Deanna turned towards them and yelled, "Yes! Calm down! He's not trying to abduct me or anything!"

Jay's attention was now on her sisters. They all shared Deanna's light skin color, body shape, and similar facial features, but unlike her, they weren't blind.

When they reached Deanna, they both stood there studying Jay like a college midterm. "Uhmm-hmmm," one of them said without opening her mouth. "And what's your purpose here?"

"He's new around here and was curious when he saw me out here doing yoga in the dark, that's all. Matter of fact, he was even nice enough to offer to walk me home before y'all showed up," Deanna answered before Jay could speak.

Jay noticed how she purposely left out the part where he thought she was the FEDs watching him. He liked that. "Yeah, I was just curious and concerned about her safety. To be honest, I just enjoyed the little time I just spent with y'all sister and would like to see her again sometime."

Her sisters looked at each other and back at him. "This little girl is only eighteen and just getting over a broken heart from a nigga using her."

"Wanda!" Deanna slapped her sister on the shoulder. "Don't be telling all my damn business!"

"Well, I literally just turned nineteen a few months ago, so her age isn't a problem for me. And no offense, but there's plenty of women I could take advantage of, but I don't. Your sister is no exception. I see something special in her," Jay informed matter-of-factly.

"Awww! That was sweet," Deanna admitted with a pretty smile.

Wanda held up her index finger, signaling for Jay to hold on, and pulled Deanna back a few feet so that they could talk some sense into her. "Girl, you don't know this damn man. Daddy's going to be pissed when he finds out you're around here talking to boys again. We're not about to go through this again."

"Oh, so I'm supposed to be alone for the rest of my life? Y'all got to stop treating me like this. It's not like the man's saying he's trying to marry me or nothing. He just wants to spend time with me, I guess. I like his energy and would like that very much," Deanna said seriously.

Her other sister, Ashley, looked back at Jay. "I don't know, sis'. It's something off about him. That man looks dangerous. It's all in his eyes and the way he carries himself."

"Is he ugly?" Deanna asked curiously.

"Well... No, he's not ugly, but..." Wanda said.

Deanna cut her off. "No, buts. Now stay y'all cock-blocking asses right here while I get finished talking to my new friend," she commanded before walking back towards Jay.

"I'll understand if you can't deal with me. After all, I am a stranger, and I don't want you to feel like a nigga trying to use you. I don't got no weird fetish or none of that crazy shit. Up until now, I never even considered sticking my dick in a blind woman," Jay said truthfully.

Deanna was turned on by his voice and his bluntness. He was pure in his own way. "I'm grown and they can't tell me who not to talk to. I have had a few boyfriends in the past who only wanted to use me for sex and hid me from everyone they knew, but that doesn't have anything to do with you. We're friends right now. I would like to spend more time with you and see the world through your eyes."

"See the world through my eyes, huh?" Jay asked amusingly. "I like the sound of that. Do you have a phone?"

She nodded and handed him a flip phone with the buttons that she could read with her fingers. "I hope you like talking on the phone because I can't really text," she joked seriously.

"I *love* talking on the phone."

Jay made his way back to the RV to check on his chicken that was fully cooked when he got back. He ate it quickly because he had somewhere else to be, and he was already running late.

From his experience, police rarely wasted their time trying to pull over motorcycles because, most of the time, they wouldn't catch a motorcycle. Jay thought it was a good idea to buy one, and he did.

He breezed through traffic on a black Kawasaki Ninja 650. He had a lot on his mind, but it wasn't overwhelming. He was confident about his position and his mission. He was currently playing an important role, which is why he chose to live a quiet life. It gave him an advantage.

About ten minutes later, he pulled up to a small unpopular park behind an insurance building. He parked his bike in front of the Escalade that was awaiting his arrival and took his helmet off. He texted Nequa's phone with an address and a time yesterday, telling her not to be late.

Nequa hopped out of the driver's seat dressed in jeans and Jordan's like the tomboy she was. She stretched lightly and made her way over to Jay, who obviously wasn't about to get off of his bike. He just sat there with both feet planted on the ground, watching her quietly.

"Word around town is that you're the man with all the answers around here," she said.

Jay shrugged his shoulders. "Not all, but most... You got a big role to play out here, so you need to be on point. It's a lot going on right now and 'a lot' had changed since you've been gone."

"Yeah, I know. Tadoe, Dizzy, and Trappa caught me up to speed for the most part, but I've been waiting for you to get in contact with me. I got a problem," she informed with a trace of uneasiness in her voice.

Jay rolled his free hand in a circular motion, signaling for her to get on with it.

"I was wondering if y'all could find somebody else to take my spot because I got a lot going on up there in Detroit. I'm not up for all this shit that's going on out here. I'm thirty-six now. I'm too old for this shit, lil' bruh."

"Well, I'm glad they caught you up to speed because you gon' have to deal with this shit. Rondo needs you and the camp needs you, so yo' ass need to sit on the throne. Look at the bright side. Rondo got faith in you. That counts for something," he informed matter-of-factly, before putting his helmet back on, speeding out of the park.

Nequa glared at him as he sped away through squinted eyes.

Chapter 16

Cleezy pumped his balls up to take a trip out to Crenshaw, California all by himself. After landing in LAX, he rented a blue drop-top Chevy Camaro and pulled up on 63rd Street off of Slawson Avenue. It was the home to the Rollin 60's Crips, the largest Crip set in the country. SVC was a branch off of this very set. They gave Cleezy the green light to paint Fayetteville blue.

There was a ground-level apartment complex that locals called The Bricks. The last time Cleezy had been out here is when he got jumped into the set. These were the type of niggas that respected a nigga with heart, and it took *a lot* of heart to do what he was doing right now.

He slowly pulled up into The Bricks, like he didn't have a care in the world. He was leaned back in his seat with his Louis Vuitton shades on, bumping Nipsey Hustle through the speakers. All eyes were on him as he navigated through the apartments and parked on the basketball court in the center of the hood.

He watched as the little homies on the block grilled him, trying to figure out who the bold niggas were that parked on their sacred basketball court. Only big homies were able to do that.

A few minutes later, a husky nigga in a blue T-shirt with a neck full of bulky jewelry walked up to Cleezy's car with a handful of little homies following up behind him. "Nigga, I don't know you, and for you, that's a big problem since you parked right here on the basketball court. Who you, C?" he asked Cleezy firmly.

Cleezy turned the music down before responding. "I C Triple-OG Cleezy Loc, reppin' that royal set, Spark Village Crips East Rollin' 60's. North Carolina line," he spat with much confidence.

The block Sergeant nodded his head. "Let me hop on the line with the big fools. Stay yo' ass right there though." He commanded, before walking back into his apartment.

The lil' homies remained on the court, loosely surrounding Cleezy's car, making sure he didn't go anywhere.

Fifty long minutes later, Cleezy was still on the basketball court. But by now, he had got out of the car and lounged on the hood. He smoked weed, shared stories, and dropped jewels on the lil' homies.

A blue Maserati truck pulled up and parked on the basketball court next to Cleezy's Camaro. Monster Loc, himself, hopped out of the driver's seat. The lil' homies hurriedly cleared the basketball court and stood guard at the outer perimeter.

"I came a long way to see this. You got to be either crazy or desperate to be out here like this by yourself," said Monster while walking up on Cleezy. He snatched the joint out of Cleezy's hand and waited for a response while puffing on the weed.

"Neither. I'm curious as to why you let your pit bull loose in my yard?" Cleezy respected Monster too much to say what he wanted to say, how he wanted to say it.

Monster smiled, showing his open-faced gold teeth. He was one of those real old-school gangsters, who used to kill the police for looking at them the wrong way. There was a reason he was at the top of the food chain. He was one helluva nigga. "Yeah, Falcon don't play no games, and I sent him because he specializes in taking shit over. Truth be told, all this shit is a test for you. If you can survive that storm, then you're worthy of your throne. If not, then you lost your grip on the streets, and it's time for you to get knocked off that muthafucka anyway... Now, pardon my back," he informed smugly before hopping back into his truck and cruising off.

He left Cleezy standing there in shock. He couldn't believe Monster was playing with his life like it was some type of game. Just a few months ago, Monster was telling him that he loved him over the phone. Now, he was trying to get him killed. The game was *cold,* and Monster had set fire to all of his winter gear, leaving him butt-naked in a nasty blizzard.

***

Falcon looked at X sideways once he walked into the spot. "Man, who the fuck is this bitch you got all up in the spot?"

"No, not bitch. The name is Jazzy Loc, nigga! And I'm one of the realest Smurfette's out here. that's why I'm all up in the spot." She retorted sassily before X could answer.

X was shocked that Jazzy had run off at the mouth at Falcon. He knew how Falcon was and was sure that Jazzy was a goner. But to his surprise, Falcon smiled. "I like this bitch. She's crazy... We need crazier around here," he joked seriously before walking to the back room.

Malik D. Rice

Chapter 17

Dizzy took a trip over to Nequa's house as soon as he got a chance. She answered the door for him but didn't let him in, so they spoke at the doorway.

"You traded on Redd before you left and he still spared your life when I told him I wanted to have yo ass whacked," Dizzy told Nequa truthfully.

Nequa sighed while running a ring-covered hand down her face. "Redd never gave a fuck about me, you, or anybody else in this city. The only reason he treated you so good is because you were out here doing all his important dirty work. Even when he got out, he was gon' continue to use you until he didn't need yo' ass no more, so don't come at me like Redd was just some righteous nigga, or something! I sided with Rondo because he has morals and had a fucking soul."

"I would whack you right now if I thought I could get away with it, but I can't. Plus, we got to work together in order to make this work, so I'm gon' put all that behind us," he said, before dropping a tied-up grocery bag, on the ground, by her feet.

"What's that?" She asked curiously.

"Yo' cut from the Crips. Don't no dues got to be paid on that money, since it's off the books, so you're good."

Nequa smiled up at him.

"Damn, I know it's a lot of money, but be cool about it. You a boss now, you can't be getting excited about shit like this," he said, with a smirk of his own.

"Boy, fuck you! This ain't my first couple of racks... I was smiling at you. I find it amusing how you fell in line with Rondo's structure after all of that shit that happened."

He shrugged his shoulders. "I'm crazy, not stupid," he retorted before leaving her alone on the doorstep.

***

"When Nequa sees the cut I'm about to bring her off of this lick, she gon' make me her Top Mafioso," Gino predicted dreamily while lying on the carpeted floor of his living room, watching the weed smoke rise to the ceiling through the rays of sun that made it through the window blinds.

Danger looked down at his son from the couch he was laying on. "I wish yo' lil' hardheaded ass would listen. This is a good score we got mapped out right here, but we really need to sit this one out. The stakes are too high. Too many risks for casualties."

"Nahhh, it's gon' be clean cut. We gon' be in and out, Pops. After this, I promise we won't have to get our hands dirty no more."

Danger gave in. "Alright. This the *last one* now!"

Gino quickly sat up with an excited expression now on his face. "This is the biggest move yet. We can't let the soldiers go on this one by themselves anyway. This shit got to go exactly as planned."

"We got the whole layout of the place mapped out, but we never discussed an actual plan. What you got on your mind, son?" Danger went along with the flow, but something deep down told him not to go through with this mission, yet he couldn't do Gino like that. He was afraid that he wouldn't be forgiven.

"Bum rush the two guards at the door and take it from there. You know, the usual drill. As long as our approach is efficient and confident, we'll come out strong. You and I will be going for the safe together though. I like how we pulled that shit off last time," Gino sounded like a proud son.

"We've got to be prepared for anything because it's not going to go down like that every time, and we got to be real fast about it because the police response time in this area is impressive."

Gino nodded his head exaggeratedly. "I'm telling you, we got this. We're built for it. Watch what I tell you."

***

Dizzy sat there and watched as Tadoe pulled out of the neighborhood. He didn't know where he was going or how long he'd be gone, so he had to hurry up and make his move.

He quickly slid on his Nike slides and took off running through the house towards the back door.

"Where you going, Dad?" Lil Dizzy asked alertly while sitting on the floor playing video games.

"I'll be right back, stay put!" said Dizzy right before disappearing out the back door.

He hopped his gate, jogged through Sasha's yard, and hopped her gate, landing in Tadoe's yard. His yard was remodeled and naturally looked better than everyone else's, but Dizzy didn't have time to admire the yard. He was on a mission.

Bang! Bang! Bang! Bang! Bang! Bang! He knocked hard on the sliding door, making sure that Persia could hear him wherever she was in the house.

"Boy, what the hell is wrong with you? Are you crazy?" Persia asked frantically with her head sticking out of an upstairs window, looking down at Dizzy. "What are you doing here, Dizzy? Tadoe will be back in a minute."

"You won't answer none of my messages or nothing. What's up with that?" he asked while looking up at her like a sad puppy.

She shook her head disappointedly. She regretted the forbidden episode she had with him. "Oh, you thought I was playing? That was a one-time thing, Dizzy. You did your job and got my rocks off that one time. It ends right there. What'd you expect? I have no future with you." She was unapologetically blunt.

"Let's see how much of a future you gon' have with Tadoe after I tell him all the shit that I did to yo' nasty ass!" Dizzy considered spitefully.

Persia shrugged her shoulders. "So. You still ain't gone have me, and you gon' be known as the nigga that kiss and tell. Bet you won't fuck another nigga's bitch after this ever again. And an evil nigga like you, I know you get off on doing shady shit like that."

"Man, fuck you! Pussy wasn't even all that good anyway. I only came back for the mouth," he lied, before making his way back to his house the same way he came.

Persia watched him in disgust while inwardly cursing herself for being weak enough to let Dizzy seduce her. She vowed to do better though.

Tadoe walked into the house with a handful of grocery bags. He took them into the kitchen and began to put the groceries away. He was rapping a song under his breath, and it looked like he was in a good mood. That made things more difficult for Persia.

She walked into the kitchen with him. "Hey, baby." She greeted timidly.

"Good afternoon, my young goddess. You missed me?" he asked, sounding happy to hear from her.

"Don't call me that because goddesses are perfect, and I'm *far* from perfect." She admitted, after leaning on the counter with her arms folded.

Tadoe stopped what he was doing and walked over to his woman. He could sense that something was wrong with her. "You're perfect in my eyes, and that's all that matters," he assured after lifting her chin with his index finger.

She pulled her face away from his grip, not wanting to hold eye contact with him. "Well, I shouldn't be... I fucked up, bae."

Tadoe gave her a sideways look, then led her to the kitchen table. He pulled out a chair for her and sat in the chair next to her. "Talk to me, lil' mamma."

Persia took a deep breath and closed her eyes. She felt like shit because Tadoe had been a good man to her all this time, and she literally shitted on him. "I fucked Dizzy a few weeks ago. It was only one time, and it was a *big* mistake. I'm so sorry, and I definitely understand if you don't want nothing else to do with me anymore," she spat rapidly in one breath. She felt relieved that the weight was off of her shoulder, but she was anxious because she didn't know how Tadoe would respond. Either way, she rather it be her that told him instead of Dizzy's bitter ass.

At first, he sat back in his chair with a blank face, digesting the information. Then to her surprise, a slow smile began to grow on his face.

"Why are you smiling? You're supposed to be cursing me out or something." That was the last reaction she expected to receive from him.

He shrugged his shoulders. "I can't really be mad at you. You know how many females that I have done did dirty in my time? I'll chalk that up as karma, but I'm not gon' keep going for that shit, Persia."

She finally made eye contact with him. "Baby, I promise it was only one time and I never planned on cheating on you again. Shit, that wasn't planned. It just happened... I'm so sorry."

"Like I said, I'm gone let that slide because I probably deserved it. Plus, you kept it real and told me yourself. I respect that, but I need to know that I don't have to worry about you bussing it open for a nigga every time yo' lil' pussy get a lil' moist."

She placed her right hand on his upper thigh. "I promise from now on, my Loyalty to you is 4Eva."

Malik D. Rice

Chapter 18

Gino, Danger, and four of their soldiers rode in the back of a windowless black van. They were on their way to their marked destination. Gangster music was blasting, and no one was talking. They were all pumping themselves up for the task at hand, and it was a very serious task.

Their target was a high-end jewelry store in Kentucky that was owned by a famous jeweler named, Hugo Duff. It was a high-risk area, but it was also an easy lick because of the location of the store. The plaza sat right by the highway, and that was a dream come true for any robber.

There was a movie theater, a shoe store, and a variety of other stores in the plaza. However, it was a Monday, so traffic was bound to be slow. They had one of the soldiers scoping the spot out for the past month and pretty much had their schedule down packed. They made weekly deposits to the bank on Tuesday, so today was the best day to hit them.

The driver took the exit and pulled into the plaza. "Alright, we need to be in and out within a matter of minutes. Same drill as the last time. Y'all four niggas clear out the shelves on the showroom floor after tying everybody up, me and Danger gon' head to the back to clear out the safe," said Gino with much anticipation in his voice.

Everyone went through the process of checking their weapons and making sure their faces were properly covered with the skull caps and bandanas.

"Something ain't right about this one, son. I feel it," Danger admitted just above a whisper and careful not to let the other men hear him.

Gino gave him the side-eye. "You just said out yo' own mouth that it was a good lick. Where that come from?"

"I don't know nigga, but I'm having second guesses right now."

"Well, I think you should go with your first mind," Gino advised, before cocking his Mossberg. "They close in ten minutes y'all. We need to be out of there in four." He opened the back door to the van, and they all spilled out.

The plaza was basically empty except for the movie theater and that was on the other side of the plaza, so they had a clear way for the most part. They approached the store from the side, so they wouldn't be spotted by security.

The four soldiers entered first, then Danger, and finally Gino.

Boom!

He fired off a warning shot into the ceiling. "Let me see them muthafuckin' hands! Any heroes *will* die today!" Gino promised while proudly watching his men round all the employees up on the showroom floor. This store was bigger than the last one, but they covered the ground with expertise like they did this a hundred times before.

He led the way towards the back of the store with Danger right on his ass. He tried to pull the door that led to the back, but it was locked. "Who got the keys to this door?" he turned around and asked.

There was no answer.

Boom!

He let off another round into the ceiling. "I said, who the fuck got the key to this door? Don't make me search y'all!"

"It-It's controlled from the management in the back. Nobody has a key," One of the employees informed in a shaky voice.

"Fuck!" Gino spat as he blew a lethal kick to the employee's head. "We got to get back there. You think they'll open the door if we start killing these hostages?" he asked Danger.

"Gino!" Danger grabbed his son's arm just as firmly as his voice sounded. "Use yo' head, son! You don't want to turn an armed robbery into a murder. Let's just get what's in the showroom and call it a day."

Gino smiled at his father while shaking his head slowly. "Too late for that, Pops. You just said my name in front of them, so they got to die anyway now," he informed calmly. "Whack 'em all!"

His men didn't hesitate to lay the employees to rest while the other two continued to clear out the shelves.

"We got to go, now!" Danger informed when he heard sirens in the distance.

All four of their bags were filled with jewelry and Gino was somewhat satisfied, so he gave the order for them to leave.

The soldiers tried to pull the doors open, but they were locked. Gino pushed them out of the way and tried to open the doors himself. "What the fuck?"

"They must've locked them from the back." Danger figured.

"It's all good! Step back!" Gino commanded before raising his gun at the glass door.

"Wooooahhh! If you shoot that door, fragments of the bullet gon' bounce back and hit yo' dumb ass! If that door locked, it's over with for us." Danger informed with a broken spirit.

Gino suddenly pushed Danger out of the way and let off a shot at the security guard on the floor, but not before the security guard could get off a shot that landed in Danger's chest.

"Awww, man! Nah, nah, nah! Damn, Pops! Breath, nigga! Breathe!" Gino said while on his knees holding Danger's head up. He was gasping for air and quickly choking on his own blood.

"How the fuck he get that gun?" Gino asked angrily.

"He got an ankle holster," one of his men answered after kicking the gun out of the security guard's hand.

"Who shot that guard, right there?" Gino asked calmly after standing back up.

The same soldier raised his hand slowly, so Gino raised his gun slowly. "I thought he was dead, bruh! I shot the nigga in the back twice!" he explained with both hands up.

"It's all good, but yo' mistake cost my father his life, so you know what it is," said Gino.

The soldier dropped his hands and took a deep breath while nodding his head up and down. Just that quick, he'd made peace with his harsh fate. It was better than spending the rest of his life in prison, so he thought about it that way and grew a smile on his face.

Boom! Gino blew him off of his feet, then walked up on him, and let off another shot at an even closer range that made his whole head disappear.

"Fuck, man!" He walked back over to Danger and took a seat back on the floor.

"What we gon' do now?" one of his soldiers asked while looking out the door at the approaching police cruisers.

Gino shot a nasty look up at him. "What the fuck you think? Either let them folks put cuffs on your wrist or shoot it out with them. Only two options you got right now, bruh," he responded harshly before focusing his attention back on his father that he'd never see again.

Out of every scenario he imagined in his head, good or bad, he never visioned things playing out like this. He didn't think his father would be torn away from him again, and he felt like he was to blame. However, his spirit was so dull to the point that he couldn't even bring himself to cry about it. It was just another wound on his scarred soul.

He rubbed a gentle hand across Danger's head before standing up. "I'm about to put them cuffs on. What about y'all niggas?"

His soldiers didn't even answer. They just stared at him awkwardly. He was standing there making jokes like his father wasn't laying lifeless at his feet. He just continued to show them more and more just how cold-hearted he really was. You couldn't fake that kind of nonchalance.

***

"I ain't even been out here for a full three weeks, and I done touched a million already. I ain't know y'all was doing numbers like this out here now," Nequa admitted truthfully.

She was kicking it with Trappa and Rod at Trappa's new house. She had to get a feel for the streets again. She wasn't going to get it back being cooped up in her mansion on the Don's strip, so she chose to hit the streets.

"Yeah, I said the same shit when I came back. The whole city done flipped," Trappa said while reemerging from the kitchen with three cold sodas in his hands.

"The shit happened quickly too. I was out here the whole time, but it was like I woke up one day and shit done flipped. We got clientele coming from all over. This the first time I saw this many people eat at once," Rod added before taking a few gulps of his soda.

Trappa turned to ESPN on the television. "Rondo did say he was gon' make it like this. Shit is crazy... It's on you right now though, Nequa. What you got planned?"

"I plan on not ending up like Donny, so I'm gon' take it easy out here," she answered seriously.

Malik D. Rice

Chapter 19

Falcon had to admit that Cleezy was holding his own, but more and more of his soldiers were running to Falcon. It was only a matter of time before the tables turned and Falcon would rule over all the Crips in the city. By then, he would have enough manpower to go toe to toe with Dilluminati. His whole mission was to take control over the Crips, so he could regain control back over the city. He made a vow to Monster, and he surely planned on keeping it.

He was laying down, deep in thought, when he heard somebody fumbling with the locks on the back door. His room was in the back of the house and his paranoia was through the roof, so he popped up and went to the window.

He saw Jazzy pacing around in the yard with her phone up to her ear, waiting for someone to answer on the other end. He was automatically suspicious because she could've just taken the call inside.

It could've just been another nigga that she was trying to hide from X, but his paranoia wouldn't let him take a chance, so he made a note to have one of his soldiers keep tabs on her. She would hear him trying to open the creaky ass window, so eavesdropping was out of the question. He got back in the bed and imagined reasons she could've been sneaking on the phone. None of them were valid.

***

"At first, I was skeptical of joining the structure. But after a while, I have seen how vital it is for our community," Tadoe admitted. "This is the first of many YF centers. I know you heard about it, but it ain't nothing like seeing it for yourself."

Nequa looked around the place in amazement. It was amazing what YF was doing for the community, and she definitely wanted parts of it. The kids in the center looked so happy. Plus, Nequa heard about the progress they were making with the junior varsity basketball team, so they mainly watched the youngins practice in the gym.

"So, these programs really getting these kids out the streets, huh?"

Tadoe nodded his head. "Hell yeah! I mean, you always gon' have the youngins that are destined for the streets, but the ones with more potential, are presented with more options."

They were entering the inside pool, where an instructor was teaching swimming lessons.

"This the type of shit I be on now. I'm all for the betterment, Tadoe. I don't want anything to do with them damn drugs. Then, on top of that, I got to deal wit that crazy ass nigga, Dizzy," Nequa vented, then shook her head in disappointment.

A wave of disgust washed over, Tadoe at the mention of Dizzy's name. As much as he didn't want to, he still felt some type of way towards Dizzy for his deceit, but he shook it off for the moment. "Don't worry about it, sis. You just got to stay out of the limelight and keep your hands clean. You should be fine."

"Better said than done. This shit overwhelming me already. I got a new respect for that nigga, Donny."

***

Donny sighed heavily, after opening his eyes to the sight of the small jail cell. He just dreamed that he was on a rooftop, at a huge party, and it was depressing to go from that to a jail cell. It didn't make matters any better that all his dreams were vivid and felt more real than the pain flowing through his veins.

They currently had him at a federal holding facility. It's where they took most federal inmates that were awaiting trial. They only had a few of these facilities in the country, so they were huge.

"Ughhh!" he grunted as he sat up on his bunk. His back was hurting from the thin ass mattress. It would definitely take some getting used to. He hoped that the mattresses were thicker wherever he ended up permanently.

He sat there and stared at the wall for a few seconds before the doors slid open. He got up and began to get himself together, so he could get his recreation time in the dayroom.

Twelve of his fellow Dilluminati brothers piled into his cell. "DG," they all said in unison, for the most part. They were from all over the country and were all there for one thing or another.

"L4E," Donny replied after spitting the toothpaste into the toilet. "Y'all ain't got to run to my cell every time the doors open. Ain't nobody dumb enough to do shit to me." He assured.

"Shittttt! If something does happen to you in here on our watch, that's all of our asses. I'd rather be safe, than sorry," Mooski countered matter-a-factly. He was a Don, from East Atlanta, and also the only other made man in the facility besides Donny.

At first, Mooski and Donny were eye-to-eye when Donny first hit the facility. However, when word got sent down that Donny got bumped up to a Capo, they started treating him even more like a God, including Mooski.

"I can't even argue with that. Let's go see what they got on this TV. We should be able to catch some of that TMZ shit," Donny said, before leading the way out of his cell.

"Yo ass might be on there *again!*" one of the Mobster's joked, drawing laughter from everybody else in the cell.

The facility was split up into six different dorms. Fifty cells on the lower and upper level of every dorm.

Donny led his men to one of the TV stations and turned to their channel of choice. They sat there and watched TV until the front door of the dorm slid open.

Four new inmates came in dragging their property on top of their mattresses. Donny's vision wasn't the best lately, so he had to squint to make sure his eyes weren't playing tricks on him.

"What the hell? I know that ain't, Gino!" he said, before popping up out of his seat and making his way towards them with his Mobsters on his tail.

It was Gino and three of his soldiers. Donny recognized them all. "Dlatt!" Donny spat as they neared.

Gino turned in their direction and grew a *big* smile on his face. "Bruh, what the fuck! You the last person I would've thought I was gon' see. I thought they had yo' ass up under the jail or some shit."

"They tried that shit, but I convinced them to surround me around the Mobsters, so I can keep 'em off the bullshit," Donny joked seriously.

"How many of y'all in here?" asked Gino.

"Seventeen now, but it was thirteen before y'all came," Donny said before instructing the other Mobsters to help them with their property.

Nobody was really in their assigned rooms. The guards let the inmates arrange their own living quarters to keep the violence down. Donny paid four niggas to move out of their rooms, so Gino and his men could be close to the rest of the team. "This whole top corner ain't nothing but DG back here. These the best rooms in the dorm. We run this whole lil' facility, and it's gon' be like that wherever we go. We all gon' end up at the same prison. It's already in the books. Anybody under Dilluminati doing FED time, got to do it with me."

"I see jail doesn't change shit. You still a young boss, my nigga. That's wassup though. I know ain't nobody complaining about that. You like the poster child for the 4's," Gino said while straightening his room out.

Donny waved him off. He was tired of the praise. "Where Danger at?"

"He ain't make it, man," Gino informed with traces of sadness in his voice. He definitely blamed himself for his father's demise. He should've just listened to him for once. He'd still be alive.

Donny made the other Mobsters wait outside the room, so he could talk to Gino one-on-one. "What happened?"

Chapter 20

"So, what you be doing for fun around here, other than listening to music and doing yoga?" Jay asked Deanna while looking around her RV. It was nice.

Her sisters must've decorated it for her. They stayed in a trailer right next to Deanna's RV. Her father agreed to let her stay in the RV by herself only if her sisters agreed to stay in a trailer text to it, so they could help her out when needed. Deanna preferred the RV because it was small and convenient for her to get around.

Jay had been talking to her on the phone every day since they met, and just like he expected, she was a unique individual. Despite her disability, she lived her life to the fullest and she didn't complain. She was a strong person, but in Jay's eyes, she was very fragile. He felt a natural urge to protect her.

"Well, I also love me some food. I can eat for days. I also like to sing too, but you're not ready for that yet," she joked seriously

Jay gave her a sideways look. "So, you've been holding out all this time."

"It hasn't been that long, Jay, and you never asked until now," she informed, after laughing at the shock in his voice.

She really was feeling him. She let her sisters help her get dressed and do her hair, so she could look good for her first visit with Jay. She felt pretty as she sat on the couch next to him.

"Can I hear you sing?" he asked nicely.

She nodded her head up and down. "Yes, you definitely can, but only if you tell me the truth about yourself... I already can't see you, so I need to know more about you."

Jay looked at Deanna hard, debating on if she was worth the effort. She was indeed a beautiful person inside and out, and he was drawn to her. It was something he couldn't quite explain, any more than he could explain why he was about to tell her what she wanted to know.

***

Dizzy swerved to a stop in front of the park in Snake Wood. Most of his Demons were in attendance. Today was a sad day in the hood. News had got around that Nasty was shot down in his car while driving by himself on the highway. That's how it was explained to Dizzy over the phone, so he pulled up to the hood to get more answers in person.

"Somebody better tell me something! Why the fuck was Nasty driving by himself? Where the fuck was y'all niggas?" he barked as he walked towards them.

It was quiet out there. The only thing that could be heard was the slight breeze that caused the drizzles of rain to fall in a slant.

"He ain't tell nobody before he left. Some of the lil' Demons said they saw him speeding out of the hood in his car by himself, and later on that night, his mamma went to tearing the house up. The Demons went to go check on her, and she said told them Nasty was dead. We don't know who it was," Crimson stepped forward and reported the news to Dizzy. He was sure to maintain eye contact.

Dizzy bit his bottom lip while glaring at Crimson savagely and took two steps closer. "Alright. You the Top Demon out here for now. But let me find out that you had something to do with Nasty's death, and yo ass is *mine* fool... Matter fact, if I even have a dream about yo' ass had something to do with it, I'm gon' whack you with my bare hands." He turned and walked back to his car before speeding off.

***

"How does a pretty little girl like yourself get mixed up in something like this? You were in *way* over your head. Donny has every agency in America after him, and you just ended up being a casualty," the US Marshal that watched over Gucci asked inquisitively.

His name was Tim, and he was the only one who she would speak to, so they made him her handler. Although they found each other very attractive, they didn't take their friendship too far. It was less complicated that way.

"I was doing just fine before I met the nigga. I guess I got greedy. Plus, looks are deceiving. I'm not innocent how you may think." She informed truthfully.

He smiled slightly. "Oh, I know you're not innocent, but I also know you're not evil like him."

Yeah, only if you knew. She thought.

"Y'all really got it in for Donny, huh? What did he do to make y'all hate him so much? I know *plenty* of scumbags on the streets that are way worse than him," she asked, admittedly taken aback.

It took a few seconds, but Tim finally answered the question. "I agree. There are worse gangsters out there, but Donny is a different type of dangerous. He has major influence and the power to touch the hearts of millions, so he has to be made an example out of. He was doing what he was doing, but also throwing it in our face. He literally taunted the government, so we nailed his ass to the cross."

Gucci shook her head. "Y'all took him off the street and all, but I don't think that's the end of him. Like you said that nigga got major reach. He can still make plenty of shit happen from that cell, including getting me whacked."

***

"Fuck all this strategy shit! Why can't I just get the bitch whacked?" Donny asked his lawyer. Her name was Camilla Carter, and she was a top-notch federal defense attorney that was appointed to his case by Dinero, himself.

Camilla shook her head frantically. "No! I promise that you'll just end up making the situation worse for yourself. There's no escaping this. The government is going to make an example out of you one way or the other. You have three options right now. You can plead guilty and take the fifteen years they're offering, you could go to trial and end up with thirty years, or you can have the star witness killed and walk. The thing is you won't make it back out of these walls. Dinero couldn't even save you from this. They will kill you if they have to. They might contaminate the air in your vents, poison your food. You never know with those slick bastards... Just take the fifteen, Donny. You'll still have a lot of life to live when you get out," she strongly advised.

"This a fucked-up system. You got child molesters, sex traffickers, and all of them type of niggas out there, but they worried about me," he complained.

Camilla shrugged her shoulders. "It's a dirty game, baby boy. Some would say you got the shit end of the stick, but it's really all about perception. You can choose to look at things in a different light. Okay, you'll have to do fifteen years in prison, but you'll be living like a king in here. You'll be surrounded by all your soldiers, you can still sell drugs in here, these female officers are going to be throwing pussy at you like nobody's business, and you're going to get out of here a very rich man. A rich man that'll still be young."

Dinero didn't respond. He just looked idly at the walls in the conference room and thought about what she was saying.

"When we go in that courtroom, you need to plead guilty and take those fifteen. You cannot beat the government, young man," she promised. "Do I need to get Dinero on the phone to tell you this himself?"

Donny shook his head *no*. "Nah, you ain't got to do all that. Fuck it, I'll take the time because you're right. I am gon' live like a king in this shit. They ain't stopping shit."

Chapter 21

Ronte stood over Manny while giving him a piece of his mind. "You slapped a radio spokeswoman in the face because she said Donny belongs behind bars? So, what! That's her opinion!"

"So! If she was bold enough to say it to my face, she was bold enough to get that ass slapped in the face!" Manny countered unapologetically.

"Yeah, now that same ass is about to sue you for a half-million dollars," Ronte retorted disappointedly.

Manny clenched his teeth as he ran a hand down his face. "I should have that hoe whacked."

"Seriously? Look at yourself, lil' bro! You losing sight of your vision, and you're losing focus. People prize you for being a positive influence on the youth, nigga! You setting the wrong example right now. I know you are upset about Donny, and I am too, but you gon' have to control your emotions. That's an order." Ronte didn't like to do it, but he had to pull rank on Manny just then.

Manny got up and stormed off into the booth. He had so many emotions built up inside of him. He needed to vent, so he did what he did best, and spoke to the mic.

Ronte sat in the chair, on the other side of the booth, at the producer's station and watched as Manny put it down on the track. He was a smart kid, with a bright future, but he still had a lot to learn. Manny was his responsibility, so he had to keep the young nigga on track.

He pulled out his phone and texted Vonte. *Tell Dinero that I said to make sure that Donny gets the lightest sentence possible. Manny's sanity depends on it, and DG Records definitely needs Manny.*

***

Nequa chose to make both Trappa and Rod her Top Mafiosos. They had what it took to lift a huge portion of the weight that sat on her shoulders. With them two in position, she wouldn't have to do much. She would only need to keep track of the incoming money.

Trappa and Rod were in a stash house looking down at four hundred pounds of demon dust, thirty bricks of cocaine, thirty bricks of heroin, and an ass-load of different prescription pills. It was the most merchandise either one of them had seen at once. They had to supply the whole camp and wholesale the rest.

"Instead of wholesaling the other half, we could only wholesale half of that half," Rod considered aloud.

Trappa looked over at him curiously. "And what we supposed to do with the rest? Nequa might be a bitch, but she's the Don now and got the power to get both of us fucked up. I'm not about to cross her, bruh."

"Hell nah, that's crazy!" Rod stated. "Instead of wholesaling the rest, we can break it down and make more money. All the extra profit could be split between us."

"I don't know. How we gon' get all that off? We already dumping the Mafiosos more than they can handle. Who gon' sale it?"

Rod grew a slow smile as he looked at his comrade.

***

Maxwell's *Pretty Wings* played softly through the speakers in Persia's room. They made a joint decision to spend a month at each house back and forth, to switch the scenery up.

Tadoe was on top of her, laying down the pipe. His thrusts matched the slow melody of the song, and Persia seemed to be enjoying herself, but Tadoe wasn't as fortunate. Her insides still felt as warm and tight as they did the first time that he'd ever been inside of her, but he couldn't stop the disturbing thoughts that plagued his mind.

He couldn't help but wonder, if she would rather fast and hard strokes, how Dizzy must've given it to her. He'd been treating her gentle and delicate, like a queen, since day one, but he couldn't help but wonder if she secretly got off by being treated like a slut.

Before he knew it, his dick began to go limp, and it only irritated him further. He pulled out of her abruptly and sat on the edge of the bed staring at the wall while breathing frustratedly.

"What's wrong, King? Did I do something wrong?" She asked, after getting up on her knees and hugging him from behind.

Tadoe shook his head. "Nah, it's really me, and my own insecurities. I can't help but think that I'm doing something wrong, that's why you must've done it with Dizzy because I wasn't hitting it right. All you got to do is tell me how you like it, and I'll make it happen."

"Baby, don't do that. He was a big mistake, nothing more. A mistake that had nothing to do with you, at all. I love the way you hit this pussy, boy. I'm not an actor, so I wouldn't be moaning if you weren't making me..."

She went on and on, reassuring him of his sexual and moral worth, but he had begun to tune her out and drifted off to his own thoughts.

Although he was in his feelings, he could still see the irony in the situation because he'd sat there and reassured many women that they weren't the reason he'd cheated on them. Now the shoe was on the other foot, and it didn't feel good. He had a new respect for scorn women. He was getting a small dose of the steady pain they endured over and over, inflicted by the very men that were meant to protect them.

He had to suck it up, chalk it up, and get it together. That was no problem, but Dizzy was still a problem. He couldn't shake the urge to touch the nigga, in some type of way, for the disrespect. He knew he should've given Dizzy a pass like he gave Persia, but it just wasn't that easy. He kept coming up with different ways to get back at the evil fucker.

Malik D. Rice

Chapter 22

Lil' Dizzy sat there staring at his father expectantly. "You still don't know who whacked Nasty? We can't let that shit slide, man."

Dizzy looked over at his ten-year-old son and could see easily how quickly he was growing up. At this rate, he would be begging to jump in the game sometime next year.

At first, that's all he wanted. The thought of his son following in his footsteps used to fill him with so much pride and joy, but not anymore. Lately, he'd been scared for his son and he wanted the best for him. He honestly didn't know what he'd do if anything happened to Lil' Dizzy, so he made a split decision right then and there concerning his future. "I'm about to send you to live in New York, with my uncle and his family. He made a good life for himself up there. Ain't nothing but failure down here for you, my son."

Lil' Dizzy shot him a mug out of this world. "Don't start that shit, man! I'm only a couple of years away from getting my Demon stamp. I'm not tryin' to go up there and live no boujie ass life. I'm from the Evil Side, and it's always gon' be in me... If you send me up there, I'm not gon' do shit but start my own gang. You might as well leave me down here, so you can look over me because yo' uncle ain't built like us."

Dizzy chuckled and shook his head sadly. As much as he wanted to stand his ground, he couldn't because Lil' Dizzy was right. The lil' nigga was too far gone and would end up like his father, no matter where he was. The apple only fell centimeters from the tree. "I can't stand yo' lil' grown-ass," he informed before slapping the shit out of Lil' Dizzy.

Lil' Dizzy looked at him with wide eyes for a few seconds, then anger quickly washed over him. He wasted no time charging Dizzy with malicious intent.

***

Meanwhile, on the north side, Falcon was sleeping real good when X woke him up. It had to be an urgent matter because X knew not to bother him, in his sleep, for anything less.

"Get up, Falc! Got the lil' nigga in the living room. He says he got something good for you too," X informed before leaving back out of the room.

It took a few minutes for Falcon to get himself all the way together. Although he was eager to hear the news, he took his time. The young nigga wasn't going anywhere.

Fifteen minutes later, Falcon emerged in the living room fully dressed, puffing on a Newport 100. "Wassup lil' nigga? What you got for me this time?"

"I just found out that them DG niggas got one of these Crip hoes working for them," Tito informed.

Falcon looked down at the youngin through squinted eyes. The lil' nigga was definitely reliable. It turned out that Blu actually trusted the lil' nigga. He was the one that tipped them that DG was assisting Cleezy in their war. Falcon knew Cleezy didn't have soldiers that could inflict that kind of damage.

That's when he did a little homework on Dilluminati and found out that Nasty was a captain in Dizzy's camp. The only camp that was capable of the bloodshed on his turf, so he had the nigga killed. Now, Tito was bringing him more information and he took it seriously.

"That's all you got?" he asked expectantly.

Tito nodded his head. "Yeah. Them DG niggas ain't drop no names, but I do know that it's a bitch and I'm betting she's on your side of the line."

"Aight, cool. I'm only gon' pay you five thousand this time because that's half-ass information," Falcon stated before nodding at X, who paid Tito and let him out of the house.

When X turned around from closing the door, he was facing the muzzle of Falcon's chrome Desert Eagle. "Woaaahhhh! What the fuck, cuz? You tripping!" X spat, still not believing what was happening.

"Nah, tender dick ass nigga! You tripping for bringing that snake ass bitch around," Falcon retorted grimly.

X wore a mask of confusion for a second, then his eyes grew wide. "Jazzy? Nah, man!"

"Yeah, nigga!" Falcon countered before removing his gun out of X's face. "Go find that bitch, now! Shit about to get real."

***

A crying Tirasia banged on Antonio's door until he answered it. Once the door was open, she flew into his arms and began to sob uncontrollably.

"What's wrong, lil' mamma? What happened?" he asked while hugging her and rubbing her head in a comforting manner.

"I was on the phone with her when the niggas kicked her door down and ran in her spot. I heard them say something about her being a slimy ass bitch and working with DG! They know she's working for somebody, so they gon' beat it out of her and she gon' drop my name. I'm a dead bitch! You've got to protect me, Tonio! You can't let them kill me!" she spat frantically.

She looked at the bags by the door. "Wait, where the fuck you going? You were about to skip town without letting me know? You knew about that?" she accused while ripping away from his arms.

"Come on, man," Antonio said while giving her a knowing look.

"Calm yo' paranoid ass down, girl! I got a photoshoot in Paris to get to and you about to come with me."

Malik D. Rice

Chapter 23

Persia was at Sparkle's sitting in Sasha's office with her head down to the floor. Sasha was a good person and would help anyone if she could. But if she was disappointed in you, she could make you feel *low*.

"I'm not saying that Tadoe a saint or nothing like that, but this the first time that nigga ever took a bitch seriously and you fucked that up. I've seen the nigga cut bitches off for looking at other niggas too long, and not only did you fuck a nigga, but you also went and fucked a nigga he knew. Congratu-fucking-lations! I should've got to know you better before I vouched for yo' ass."

"I didn't ask you to vouch for me. I got mad respect for you and all, but you not gon' sit here and make me feel worse than I already feel. Plus, I owned up to my shit and kept it real. I'm not perfect and neither is Tadoe, so stop making it seem like he's just a saint or something," Persia shot back, after picking her head up, and glaring at Sasha.

Sasha scooted up on top of her desk and took a deep breath. "I'm not saying that Tadoe is perfect. I just never seen the nigga care and try this hard, about a relationship. He's finally at that point in his life where he's ready to settle down, and I think you just fucked that up, girl."

"Damn! Why life got to be so damn complicated?" Persia asked frustratedly.

Sasha shrugged her shoulders. "I don't know, girl. It just is. But like you said, you're not perfect and Tadoe knows it, which is why he forgave you. I don't know if he forgave Dizzy. That nigga is territorial as fuck."

***

Cleezy sat on the steps in his safe house located on the outskirts of the city. His head was down in between his legs, his eyes were shut tight, and he clenched his teeth so hard that his nerves were rattling. He was trying hard not to lose his cool.

Blu had just shown up and dropped a *big* bomb on him. Word was going around that Cleezy and Blu, were officially traitors of the Crip nation. Word got all the way out about their dealings with DG, how they conspired with them, and assisted in the death of nearly a dozen Crips. Cleezy tried to call Monster to save face, but Monster wasn't trying to hear that shit. They were done for.

"Listen, Cleezy. I know it seems like a bad and hopeless situation right now, but I think I got a solution to all of our problems," Blu pitched intensely.

Cleezy looked up at his right-hand-man, with a knowing look. He felt like it was a hopeless situation, but they had nothing to lose, so he heard Blu out. "What's the magic plan, Genius?"

Blu stuck a cautious hand out towards Cleezy. "Okay, hear me all the way out before you discredit what I got to say... We got plenty of loyal soldiers that will follow us to the end of the earth. If they'll follow us that far, then they'll definitely follow us to the other side."

Cleezy continued to stare at him with a blank face but didn't say a word, so Blu went further. "When you really think about it, it's not a bad idea at all. Crip turned their backs on us, so we could just take our soldiers and convert to YF. I know some of our soldiers would be reluctant to go DG because of the tattoos and the history, but they basically love that YF shit. If we can convince them to stamp us YF, then we'll really be tied in with Dilluminati, and the odds will be turned against Falcon's bitch ass."

"Damn... That's actually a good idea, Blu."

***

Donny received his own personal visitation room and hours. Antonio sat there and waited for his comrade to emerge. He had a bunch of food and snacks from the vending machine laid out on the table for Donny.

Donny walked into the room in free-world clothes and a body full of jewelry. Antonio was openmouthed. "Damn, nigga! I was expecting you to come out here in an ugly ass uniform, smelling like a dumpster, but you in here dabbing! How the hell you do that?"

"You watch too much TV, man," Donny joked, before taking a seat at the opposite end of the table. "They let me wear whatever I want, as long as it's all white like the dress code. They let me do whatever the fuck I want as long as I keep the violence down, and don't try to escape."

Antonio shook his head. *Only Donny* "How you been feeling though. I see you living it up in here, but I know that shit probably hard for you to be in this muthafucka."

"Mannnnn. It ain't even about this prison shit. It's the reason I'm in here, that got me feeling some type of way. All these secret deals being made behind doors, and shit. You would think that street niggas are the most cutthroat individuals in America, but it ain't us. It's the government. They play some dirty games, bruh."

"What happened?" Antonio asked curiously.

Donny wanted to tell him about how it was them that leaked the sex tape and the threats of them having him killed if he fought his case, but he decided against it. It wouldn't solve anything, and there was nothing Antonio could do about it anyway. "Don't worry about it. What's up though? You good out there? How's that modeling shit been treating you?"

"The legitimate life is treating me well, but fuck all that..." Antonio looked around the room and lowered his voice. "You think they listening to us right now?"

Donny shook his head. "I already took my time. I'm federal property now. As long as I'm in here, they are not worried about me. Tell me what you got to tell me."

"Mannnn!" Antonio sighed, then continued. "My bitch sent one of her friends at Falcon to get the drop on the nigga, but he found her out. Now shit is all fucked up. I got my bitch living with me and Cleezy got the boot from the big Crips out in Cali."

Donny showed shock on his face. "Damn... That's crazy."

"That's what I said, but Cleezy approached Dizzy with a proposition and Dizzy reached out to me, so I could come run it across you."

Donny rolled his hand impatiently, signaling for Antonio to get along with it already.

"Cleezy said that he got over thirty loyal men and he trying to convert over to YF. He already discussed it with his men, and they're with it. They're just waiting on your green light."

Donny sat back in his seat and poked his lip out while considering the request. It wasn't too bad of an idea. In fact, it was a power-move on both ends. Since Antonio was out of the streets, YF had kind of gotten watered-down. With Cleezy, and his men, added to the brand, it was a big win. Plus, he could still run operations from his cell. It was genius.

"Tell Cleezy that under normal circumstances, I would make him pay $400,000 upfront for this favor, but I know his money good and I know what he capable of. I'm gon' grant his request and stamp him. He's gon' be the President, but he will report to *me* and me only. I'm about to get transferred to my permanent prison in a few days, where I'll have a phone waiting on me. I'm gon' give you the number to give to him. We gon' get rid of that nigga Falcon once and for all, then we gon' get to this money. But he better make sure he pays them dues on time, every time. Other than that, tell that nigga to breathe easy. He well connected, protected, and soon to be respected."

Donny looked at Antonio nodding his head in understanding but was skeptical. "Do you need to write that shit down, nigga? It's an important message, and if you fuck it up, I'ma have you fucked up!"

"You got a pen?" Antonio asked in a playful manner.

Donny exhaled hardly, but it came out like a monstrous grunt. He got up out of his chair and knocked on the door to borrow a pen and paper from one of the guards.

Chapter 24

Dinero had a real octagon Mixed Material Arts ring in his gym. Vonte had been grooming him to become a lethal weapon, and that came with hand-to-hand combat. They trained a few days out of the week. Either in the gym or on the firing course. Dinero was a quick learner and dedicated to anything he put his mind to.

Vonte sent a roundhouse kick Dinero's way, and he ducked it. When he came back up, he took a huge step back.

"Stop running from me, twin. I told you about that shit." Vonte commanded in frustration.

Dinero came forward, with a series of strategic punches, then backed back up. "Don't tell me how to fight, nigga. I'm gon' take what you teach me and create my own style."

"That's why you ain't gon' never beat me!" Vonte spat.

He'd been kicking the whole time and Dinero was definitely anticipating a kick, so he faked one. When Dinero's eyes left him, he leaped forward with a flying punch to Dinero's head that dropped him instantly.

The lights went out for Dinero, but not for long. His eyes were back opened within seconds, and he saw a smiling Vonte, standing over him. "Help me up, nigga. Felt like God was descending down on a nigga just then."

Vonte took his hand, to pull him up, but Dinero snatched away. He suddenly adopted a distant look on his face. "What's wrong with you?"

"I got it!" Dinero exclaimed excitedly.

"Got what?"

"The meaning behind DG4... Descendants of God! That fits the description of the society perfectly."

Vonte rolled his eyes inwardly while looking down at him sideways. "So, what the 4 stands for?"

"4Eva."

Vonte nodded. "Well, you need to be thanking me because if I would've never knocked you out, you would've never come up with that shit."

"Fuck you, nigga!" Dinero spat, before clipping Vonte's legs, causing him to trip to the floor. Once he was on the floor, Dinero jumped on top of him, and they started grappling on the ground, struggling to put each other in a submission.

***

Jay looked down at, Deanna, who laid on him. Her legs were up on the couch, and her head rested in his lap. He ran his hands through her soft hair, and watched the television, while she listening to it. Kevin Hart was acting a straight fool on the stage.

"He so damn funny." She admitted jokingly.

Jay looked down at her, with a smile. She was so beautiful inside and out, and he really enjoyed her company. He couldn't remember the last time he actually took a girl seriously and would've *never* known that the one he did take seriously would turn out to be a blind woman. It's crazy because he didn't care about all that. It just made her more fragile, and precious towards him. "Yeah, that nigga a trip. His short-ass plays too damn much," he informed playfully.

Deanna sighed. "You're a very interesting person, and now that you've told me all the stuff you did, I feel bad that I can't do any of those things with you. Don't get me wrong, I highly appreciate you spending time with me and keeping me company, but I know you get bored sitting inside, watching TV, and listening to music all day." She didn't seem insecure, just concerned. For him.

"Please, stop that shit shawty. That's really why I didn't want to tell you all about me, but you wouldn't let up. I told you because I trust you, for some reason, and I know you really wanted to know more about me, but I didn't tell you so that you can feel bad." He leaned down and placed a soft kiss on her forehead. "So, like I said, stop that shit. I'm laying low and would've had this lifestyle change anyway. I'm just glad that you're in the picture. You good for a nigga soul."

"Now, that's how you reassure a bitch right there!" She joked, causing him to laugh.

His phone began to vibrate in his pocket, and she sat up, so he could access it. He fished his phone out of his pocket and looked at the screen. It was Rondo. He answered immediately. It was a video call, so it automatically went on speaker. "Been a minute, nigga. How you?"

Rondo chuckled. "I'm good. Been working as usual, but it's paying off tremendously. How're things out there?"

"Everything and everybody's still in place. Nequa's adjusting to her position, and we took over the west side. Cleezy got the boot from the Crips, for being in cahoots with us, so he just took his soldiers and went YF, since it would've been kind of weird if they turned DG. It's really a lot going on out here, but not bad enough that I had to step in. They got it covered, plus Donny playing the Capo position from behind the wall, making my job easier." said Jay.

"That's wassup. As long as the structures still in place... How have you been though? I know how much you love the action, but I can't honestly afford to lose you, so I'm gon' need you to continue laying low until shit dies down."

Jay nodded his head. "Believe it, or not, I'm not even tripping. I found something to occupy my time."

Deanna smiled.

"You mean someone? Who is it? She got to be one helluva hoe to deal with you, nigga." Rondo joked seriously, with a big smile, flashing his new veneers.

Deanna's frowned.

"She's not a hoe, nigga. Her name is Deanna, and I'm actually treating this one right, so she not having no problems dealing with me," said Jay matter-a-factly.

Rondo's mouth dropped, and his shocked expression turned into an even bigger smile. "Where she at? I got to meet the girl that got you like this. I don't believe it!"

"Here." Jay didn't even hesitate to give Deanna the phone, and her smile had returned. Even brighter this time.

"Oh my God! You're a beautiful, young lady. I can see why Jay is like that over you," Rondo said truthfully.

Deanna knew about Rondo before she even met, Jay. She loved listening to Manny, and Manny wouldn't let you forget him. She was honored to be talking to the legend, and she had Jay to thank for it. "Thank you, Sir."

"No, I thank you for calming that lil' nigga down. He can be a real wrecking ball when he wants to, but I can already see that he's delicate around you. That's basically a miracle... Malika, look at this shit. Jay done found a *sweet* girl, and he actually treating her with some respect."

Malika rushed to the phone and looked down at a still smiling, Deanna, on the screen. "Danggg! She's pretty as hell, and natural too. You go, girl! I'm sorry, I look a mess right now."

"I wouldn't know. I can't see anyway." Deanna retorted, but she actually spoke faster than she intended, and suddenly tossed to phone over at Jay.

Jay chuckled and picked the phone up. "My bad. She just a lil' shy, but yeah, she wouldn't know because she's blind y'all. She can't see y'all, she just knows what I done told her about y'all," she stated truthfully.

Deanna looked his way, in total shock. She had butterflies in her stomach and was breathing short breaths. Her anxiety was through the roof.

"Oh, I'm sorry!" Malika spat apologetically.

Jay waved her off. "Nothing to be sorry about. She's a good girl, and I'm glad I met her. She in good hands, and y'all know that, so no need to feel sorry for her."

"I'm proud of you, Jay. I see your growth bro'. We gon' leave y'all to it though. Take it easy. I'll be in touch when I get a chance." Rondo promised, before ending the call.

Jay looked over at, Deanna, who still sat there uneasily. "As far as I'm concerned, that's the only family I have in this world. I'm not ashamed of you, and I'm not ashamed of us."

Deanna felt beautiful emotions flowing through her body, and it felt good. Jay was a real nigga, and he was bringing extreme joy into her life already. Little did he know, he basically had her heart in his hand already, he just hadn't closed his hand around it yet.

She didn't even respond verbally. Instead, she reached both hands out for his face, and when she found it, she pulled him in for a long kiss. Their first *real* kiss and it sparked a blissful flame in them both.

Her breathing got heavier and she started kissing him sloppier, but he pulled himself back. "Nah, not like this. You don't have to do this just because I did that. I still want to take shit slow how we been doing. You a princess, and I'm gon' continue to treat you like it. We'll cross that line when the time is right."

"Where you been all my life?" She asked, after a long sigh.

Jay placed his arm around her shoulder, and puller her in close. "On my way here. Took a minute, but I'm here." He kissed her forehead and focused back on the television. He hadn't felt this much inner peace, ever, in his young life.

Malik D. Rice

Chapter 25

It was *Throwback Thursday* night at Blast Off. The older generation, in the city, gathered there to skate, and have a good time. Cleezy was in that generation and planned on showing up anyway, so he decided to kill two birds with one stone, by calling a meeting with his new comrades.

"Dawg, look. That lady out of control." Blu informed, then noted, while pointing toward the pool tables.

Cleezy looked and shook his head. It was his ex-wife. She left him, a few years ago, because she felt that he loved the streets more than he did her. She'd been bouncing from man to man ever since, trying to find love.

He watched as she leaned over the pool table in a skimpy skirt, with a heavyset older man behind her, *trying to show her how to shoot.* "That lady ain't none of my concern. Fuck her."

"That's right. Where these niggas at?" Blu asked impatiently.

Cleezy nodded his head at the entrance. "You might want to take that *S* off of *niggas*."

Dizzy, and Nequa, walked into the building and quickly found Cleezy's VIP section. They had to walk around the skating ring, to get to the section, but they eventually made their way.

"Throwback Thursday night? Really? This ain't my steelo," Dizzy asked after taking his seat. Nequa sat beside him.

"Well, it's mine. Plus, it's a good vibe in here with these older cats. Don't got to worry about no reckless young niggas shooting up the place." Cleezy countered matter-a-factly.

Nequa nodded her agreement. "I agree. I have never been in here on a Thursday, but it's definitely a different vibe. I think I like it."

"I don't think we had the pleasure of meeting. I go by the name of Blu. Vice President of YF," Blu only introduced himself like a gentleman to a woman he considered worthy, and the amazon sitting across from him was definitely that. Black, skinny niggas like him, loved a light-bright big woman, any day.

He could tell that she wasn't girly, by the way, she carried herself, and she was even a little on the thick side, but it still didn't take from the fact that she was pretty. She was his type. He looked her up-and-down openly admiring her attire that was similar to his, and the way she wore her long box braids wasn't like a lady, but they still looked good on her. The fact that she still had traces of feminism inside of her, was all it took for him.

"Nice to meet you, Blu." Nequa returned the greeting with a smile. "My name is, DG Nequa, and I'm a Don Diva."

Blu returned the smile. "I've heard of you; I just didn't know you were this pretty. I would've been crossed enemy lines to find you, girl."

Nequa blushed and she began to soften, as her panties began to moisten a little. It's been a while since she had some actual dick, and just the thought of getting some did something to her.

"If y'all are done tongue-fucking each other, we got business to tend to." Dizzy spat, before turning towards Cleezy. "Wassup, old man? What you call this meeting for?"

"Just want to be on the same page with y'all since we in the same boat now. Y'all stood for something else when DG came along, and YF is no different. It's something new for me, and my guys, but we'll make it work."

Nequa nodded. "I understand."

"You got Dilluminati behind you now, but that doesn't change shit. Yo' soldiers still gon' have to put in some work. Hustling on the block and slanging that Glock." Dizzy added. "Any word about, Falcon."

"Nah, man. We're still trying to figure out how the hell they found out about the bitch y'all had on Falcon. I ain't tell nobody but my lil' cousin, and I know he ain't gon' do no shit like that... Who you tell about that, Cleezy?" asked Blu.

Cleezy looked at Blu and shook his head from side to side rapidly. "I don't talk to people about shit like that."

"You might need to check on yo' family, Blu. That doesn't mean shit these days. Folks will cross you for the smallest reason. Family or not."

Blu clenched his teeth, and nodded his understanding, hoping that Lil' Tito didn't do that shady ass shit.

***

When Falcon learned of Cleezy's little *power move*, he pulled an ace out of his own sleeve. He called back to California and requested an army of his own, and of course Monster consented. At first, his only job was to overthrow Cleezy and take his throne, but now his sentence was death. The ultimate cost of betrayal.

He paced the ground in front of nearly two dozen thoroughbred soldiers, that were straight off of the road. They'd traveled a long way, and were likely tired, but there was no time for rest. They didn't come for that.

"Right now, we got the upper hand. They think I already lost this lil' war, but they gon' have another thing coming. We gon' hit these folks where it hurt." Falcon chanted, with fire in his voice.

"And where is that?" One of the soldiers asked.

Falcon stopped pacing and faced the soldier. "I got a crack in their infrastructure. I'm going to find out where they're holding their drugs, and we gon' hit their pockets. That's what's going to hurt them the most."

X walked up to Falcon after his little speech. "You really think we got a chance. I mean, me and you done been through some shit, and we done took over a lot of shit, but I just got a feeling we need to finish Cleezy off and head back to the Mother Land. Monster don't care about Fayetteville no more. He just wants Cleezy's head. We can definitely handle that task, but I don't know about the other one."

"I care about Fayetteville!" Falcon spat firmly while getting in X's face. "And I will take over this city. With or without you. After Cleezy's head is on a stick, nigga. This ain't our first time against the odds, nigga. You been riding with me this long, don't bitch up now. Pardon my back." Falcon advised, before walking off towards his car.

X swallowed the lump in his throat and breathed deeply through his nose while watching Falcon walk off. He couldn't *bitch up*, so he followed.

Malik D. Rice

Chapter 26

Blu went to his aunt's apartment in Spark Village. She was a nice woman, with a lot of appealing characteristics about herself, so Blu couldn't see how she created a fat lousy nigga like Tito. He had to be a splitting image of his sperm donor.

"Hey, Blu! Come on in. It's been a minute since you visited your auntie." Tito's mother, Neesha, greeted brightly, but the smile was gone when she turned around from closing the door. "What did Blu do? He's been having all this extra money lately and when I asked about it, he told me to keep quiet about it. If you're here without your mother, he must be in some type of trouble."

Blu looked at Neesha real hard. Most of the love he had for Tito came from her. If it wasn't for her, he probably would've killed Tito a while ago, for some of the other bullshit he's pulled in the past. "He fucked up bad this time, Auntie."

She saw the seriousness in Blu's eyes, and her eyes grew large. She feared this day for a long time. Tito had fucked up ultimately, and she was very much scared. Tito was a dickhead, but he was her only child, and she couldn't help her love for the little bastard.

She took a big step closer to, Blu and looked into his eyes with pure desperation. "Nephew, please listen to me! Now, I need you to fix this. Please. Just do it for me. I know him being your cousin might not mean too much to you right now, but I'm your favorite aunt, and he's my *only* child. Please spare him this one last time."

Blu shook his head from side to side sadly. He couldn't even hold eye contact with her. He wanted to do this for her so bad, but there were rules, and Tito has broken them one, too many, times. "This is bigger than me, Auntie. He's supposed to be a dead man right now, and Cleezy was prepared to do it himself because he knew I could never, but fortunately, I convinced him to seek a lesser punishment."

"He has to leave the city for good, huh?" she asked expectantly.

Blu nodded.

"Thank you so much, Nephew!" she said before hugging him tightly, for a few long seconds. "I'm about to go wake him up and make him go pack his shit now! He'll be out of the city in a matter of hours!" She promised. She already knew where she'd send him, and all.

Blu shook his head. "Nahhh, Auntie. First thing's first, he has to get violated the hard way, then he has to undergo a full interrogation. He's involved in some deep shit, and I'm just as devastated as you are, but this is a slap on the wrist compared to what he's supposed to get."

Neesha nodded her understanding. "I can't even argue with that. Well, he's in the back. I guess you can go get him."

"Nah, it's going down in here. It's an urgent matter," he informed, before reaching in his pocket and handing her a handful of twenties. "That's for the inconvenience, but I'm gon' need you to leave for a few hours. When you come back, you can get him ready to leave town."

She didn't say another word. She just rushed into the back room, to grab her purse, and quietly left the apartment, with tears in her eyes.

Two minutes later, Blu's enforcers walked through the apartment door. They were three of the toughest niggas out of the whole set. Blu led them back to Tito's room, where he was sound asleep.

He had on a pair of basketball shorts, and a tank top, sprawled out on top of the covers. Blu flipped on the light switch, as one of the enforcers grabbed one of Tito's legs and yanked him off the bed, down to the floor, where they proceed to hand him an ass whooping of a lifetime.

"Bruh, what the fuck! Come on, man! Ahhhhh! Ah-ah-ahhhh! Aw-www-shit!" Tito's cries for help, turned into mumbled muffles, as he balled up in a fetal position.

When the stopwatch on Blu's phone reached forty-four seconds, he stopped them and walked up to Tito. He was pretty fucked up, and probably would need to spend the night in the hospital before he left town, but he would live.

"You gon' tell me *everything* you know about Falcon, and them niggas, or I'm gon' let these niggas get a round two on yo' ass," he informed coldly, as he bent down over, Tito.

***

Rod convinced Trappa to go along with his plan of operation. They were loyal to the structure, but they had to play for keeps if they wanted it all to be worthwhile. The money they originally were making from their cut didn't quite add up to the risk they were taking, by trafficking all of that weight. The only way they would be able to pull it off was expansion. Unofficially of course.

They were on the way to go meet with their first clients. Rod sat in the driver's seat of the van, bumping his head to the music, and Trappa sat in the passenger's seat, on the phone arguing with his baby's mother.

"You dead ass wrong, Tia! You moving this nigga in already? You barely know the fuckin' nigga! I know I ain't perfect, but everything I did, I did for us. You really shitting on a nigga right now. I don't deserve this!" he barked into the phone. His anger was evident.

Tia sucked her teeth. "I didn't deserve most of the shit you put me through, but that's life. He's a good man and plans to take care of us properly. I deserve a man like him, Trappa. Instead of being all selfish, and shit, try to be happy for someone else, for once in your life." She reported calmly, before ending the call.

Trappa heard the click, and pulled the phone away from his face, to look at it. "Stupid! ass! bitch!" He banged the phone on the dashboard, with every word, and the screen broke from the last blow. He then rolled the window down and tossed the phone out of the window.

"You know if the state troopers would've seen that they would've pulled us over, right. You need to chill out. We got some important business ahead of us. You can cry about Tia later." Rod advised, after glancing in Trappa's direction.

An hour later, they were driving through a very small town in North Carolina that was about forty minutes outside of Goldsboro. A pickup truck met them in Goldsboro and had to escort them the remainder of the way because a GPS wouldn't take them there. The place had no official address. it was literally off of the map.

There was a huge patch of woods that stretched out to a fifteen-mile radius in all directions. In the middle of that patch of woods was a whole rundown community.

"What the fuck?" Trappa spat shockingly, as the narrow dirt road opened up to a whole neighborhood.

"I found out about these folks from my cousin. He fucked around and got one of these bitches pregnant. That's the *only* reason he knows about the place. About seven families moved out here about two hundred years ago, and started they own lil' community." Rod informed while taking in the uniqueness of the place himself.

Trappa snobbishly turned his nose up. "That's some real country ass shit. Look at these folks. Real backwoods rednecks."

"Hell yeah, they are, but they go hard. These white boys out here crazy, so you need to watch what you say around them, nigga. I'm trying to make it up out of here," Rod scolded seriously.

The pickup truck rode to the heart of the community, where a lot of commotion was going on. A large group of rowdy white boys crowded around a big ditch.

Rod and Trappa hopped out of the car and met up with the driver of the pickup truck. He was a super-skinny white man, with yellow teeth, and a Mohawk that matched. "Welcome to Americus! Our little slice of heaven!" He greeted enthusiastically.

"This supposed to be heaven?" Trappa asked unpleasantly.

Rod nudged him with his elbow, signaling for him to shut the fuck up. "What's going on out here? Lil' dog fight?" He changed the subject swiftly.

"Dogs! Oh nooo! We fight 'gators 'round here... Come on! Let's go get us a closer look!" Yellow Teeth informed excitedly, in his deep southern drawl, before quickly leading the way over to the crowd.

Trappa looked at Rod with wide eyes. "You got us out here with these psychotic ass white boys, and shit. If we get killed, I'm gon' kill you again in the afterlife." He promised seriously.

"Aight, Killa. Now, come on, so we can get this over with." Rod stated playfully, before following Yellow Teeth.

Both Rod and Trappa watched the alligator fight in amazement. The two baby gators were going at it like rival enemies.

A strong hand closed on Rod's shoulder, and it startled him so much, that he jumped involuntarily. "What the fuck?" He spat, after turning around, with a nasty mug plastered on his face.

"That's my fault, bud. Didn't mean to startle you there. I'm, Bubba. The Mayor of, this here, city of ours." A big, tall, and bald, white man greeted warmly.

Rod and Trappa looked up at the Terminator looking-ass-nigga silently, but it was Trappa that spoke. "Why y'all choose to live all the way out here?

"Wasn't us. It was our ancestors that established, this here, fine piece of land. We just built on it and expanded. This is home for all of us." Bubba answered matter-a-factly.

"That's what's up, and as much as I would like to sit here and learn the history of this place, we have a tight schedule, so I'd like for us to get down to business. I mean if that's not a problem for you Mr. Mayor." Rod stated seriously.

Bubba nodded his approval, and signaled for them to follow, after walking off. He led them to the only trailer in the whole community. There was a big sign on top of the trailer that read *Mayor's Office*.

Bubba led them inside, and it was really set up like an office. "This is where the citizens come to file complaints, come for loans, jobs, counseling. I do it all for my people, and that Demon Dust y'all got, will help with a lot of plans, and problems, that we have around here. People are smoking it uncut. It's strong enough to substitute heroin, and that's miraculous. It'll literally save a lot of my people from that monkey on their backs. I much rather they be hooked on Demon Dust, it's just like weed."

Rod and Trappa remained standing, while Bubba sat on top of his desk. They were eye-to-eye now. "How much can you handle? We basically have an unlimited supply." Rod informed while rubbing his hands together in a prayer position.

"Uhmmmm, about fifteen pounds every two weeks. I'll have to build a clientele first, and I can pay for that right now."

Rod looked at Trappa, and back at Bubba. "Deal." It was perfect because they were taxing Bubba nearly three times the normal price. It was as if they were breaking it down.

Nobody around Bubba's vicinity had more than an ounce of Demon Dust, so with fifteen pounds, he would control the market, which is why he didn't have a problem paying their prices. It was a win-win for both parties. Everyone was happy.

Chapter 27

Donny ended up at Leavenworth U.S Penitentiary in Leavenworth, Kansas. It's one of the most violent prisons in the country and they accepted Donny into their *fine* institution for a reason.

They were forced, by the governor, to let half of the inmates out of isolation, and allow them to live in a general population amongst one another. They believed that Donny could keep the drama down, and there was a lot of drama at Leavenworth, so Donny had his hands full.

His first week there, there was some *major* transferring that took place. The biggest wave of prison transports that America has ever seen. There were approximately 214 members of Dilluminati spread throughout the federal penal system in the country. He saw to it that every last one of them was transferred to the prison with him. After his army was in place, everything else slowly began to fall into place.

There were Godfathers and Popes at the prison with Donny, but everybody knew who ran the show. Donny was high-powered, and nobody disputed that. There were also heavy hitters from other organizations, and crews, that he had to acknowledge, if the peace treaty would work, so he called a meeting with all of them in the prison's basketball gym. They stood in a circle at the center of the basketball court.

"One thing about it, we all got to live in this muthafucka together. Why not unite? Because the government already fucked with us, when he passed the law, enabling eligible prisoners to live in general population, but if shit keeps going how it been going, then y'all gon' make him look bad, and I don't think that's a good idea. Everybody standing in this circle has the power to get a lot of shit done, but imagine what we could accomplish if we came together."

All eyes were on him, and as he scanned the small crowd, it seemed as everyone was paying close attention to what he had to say, so he continued. "I already had a talk with the warden. He'll make the administration stay out of our way if we keep the violence down. There's only six hundred prisoners in population, and over two hundred of them mine. I can control mines, but the question is, can y'all control yours?"

They all nodded in unison.

"Good! We got an understanding. To keep shit established, and solid, we'll meet right here every other week to make sure everybody on the same page. If you standing right here, right now, then you part of the roundtable. Fuck administration! We run this camp now. All we got to do is stand united... On another note, I got a *big* shipment of phones and Demon Dust on the way. That should make these niggas sit down somewhere. I'll make sure all of y'all receive a decent bundle to feed the wolves, but you'll have to buy anything extra."

After the meeting, the other big homies left out of the gym with their security, but Donny stayed. The warden wanted to have a quick word with him before he went to his counselor's appointment.

"How'd it go? Looks like you all are on one page." Mr. Ridge asked, then stated, after walking up to Donny. He was a slim Caucasian man, with a Johnny Depp hairstyle.

"I told you, I got this shit. Just let me rock how I rock, and you won't have no problems. Stay out of my way, and I'll stay out of yours. I'll have the same amount wired into your account every four months. You gon' retire a very rich man." Donny informed, before walking off with twenty-four Mobsters surrounding him.

Mr. Ridge watched as the young tycoon walked away with his entourage. He'd never shown this much favoritism to any inmate before, but Donny was different. Plus, he paid well, so as long as he stayed inside of the gates of Leavenworth and kept the violence rate down, he was basically free to do whatever the hell he wanted.

The lobby of the counselors' office wasn't too big and there were already a dozen prisoners inside waiting to see their counselors, so Donny waited outside with his men because there was no way they would all fit inside.

They were outside kicking it like they were on the block. Laughing, talking shit, and smoking weed, like they didn't have a care in the world.

"Come on, Donny. It looks like you about to shoot a damn rap video out here." The Unit Manager over the general population stated as he walked up to them.

Donny didn't put his joint of weed out, like his comrades, but he did have enough respect to cuff it behind his back. "We had to post up out here. From now on, y'all gon' have to schedule me my own counseling session because my security going with me *everywhere*."

The Unit Manager nodded his head in agreement. "I'll see to it. But you gon' have to let me get a picture with you since you already picture-ready and shit," he joked seriously while pulling his phone out.

The government kept their end of the deal. They transferred all of his men, and they basically allowed him to do whatever he wanted, as long as he didn't try to escape. That came with a mean wardrobe. He had on Rock & Republic jeans, Prada shoes, and a button-down Burberry shirt. That along with all the new jewelry, Manny, had donated him. He was picture-ready.

The Unit Manager snapped a few pictures, and checked them out, with a big smile. "Yeah, my kids gon' love this!" he admitted before walking off.

Donny just shook his head, with an amused smirk on his face, while exhaling weed smoke.

Twenty minutes later, the warden walked past Donny and his men. "What's going on?"

Donny stepped up, from the wall of his men, so he could be seen. "Waiting for these folks to get finished so I can see my counselor. Y'all gon' have to start scheduling me my own sessions. We can't fit in that lobby with all of them other niggas."

The warden nodded his agreement before walking into the counselor's lobby.

A few minutes later, he emerged holding the door for the inmates that were waiting to see their counselors. Some of them looked very unpleased, that their appointment was being rescheduled, but they'd live.

After the lobby was clear, Mr. Ridge signaled for Donny to enter. "I can't have y'all on my front walk loitering and smoking. This is a front street where my visitors come, so just try to make me look good, now."

"I got you, Unc. You don't be smoking weed? I got some good shit for you?" Donny asked half-jokingly.

"Enjoy your appointment, Donny," Mr. Ridge said before walking off.

***

Donny was sitting down, listening to music through his earbuds that were connected to his phone. He had enough respect for the administration, not to pull it out in the lobby, but he had to have his music. He was in his own little world, with his eyes closed, so he didn't see his counselor, or hear when she called his name.

"Donald Redfarn!" she called again, a little louder than the first time.

"He can't hear you because he listening to music, but even if he could, he wouldn't answer you. He only answers to Donny," one of the Monsters informed matter-of-factly.

She proceeded to go tap Donny herself, but ten of the Monsters stepped forward with their chests out.

"We can't let you do that."

Another Mobster tapped Donny on the shoulder, and he took one of his headphones out. "Wassup?"

"This lady was calling yo' real name, but we were telling her that you only answer to Donny."

Donny pulled his phone out and paused the music before standing up and locking eyes with the most beautiful woman he'd seen since he'd been locked up. He walked past his men until he was face-to-face with the well-dressed goddess. "She can call me whatever the hell she wants... You gon' lead the way to your office?"

The counselor eyed him up and down, unable to hide her approval, and just walked off without a word.

Donny leaned his head sideways, to get a good look at her round ass. "Two of y'all stand in front of the door, while I'm in there. The rest of y'all post up out here," he commanded, before following the ass down the hallway.

After Donny was seated in the office, on the other side of the counselor's desk, he studied the beautiful brown chocolate, sitting in front of him. "Is that your real hair and eyes?"

"Yes, it is, but that's beside the point. You're here for a counseling session. Let's get on with it. I'm Ms. Pitts, your permanent counselor. How are you adjusting to the prison life?" she asked seriously.

"Donny held his hands out. How does it look like I'm adjusting? Ain't shit change. The only thing I can't do in here is drive a car. Other than that, life must go on."

Ms. Pitts nodded her head. "I'm sure you have every female administrator under your fingernails. I'm trying to figure out why Manny went through all that trouble to get me to work down here. Seems like you got everything you need."

"What!" Donny spat, with a slow-growing smile approaching. "That sneaky ass nigga. You one of Manny's girls?"

"Uhmm, no. I was a very successful Psychiatrist before this. He walked into my office one day with just as many men behind him that you have with you now and offered me an awful amount of money to come here and work as a counselor. Your counselor," she informed matter-a-factly.

Donny licked his lips and rubbed his hands together in a prayer position. "Is that right? I'm gon' have some real fun with yo' lil' ass."

"Boy, please. He only paid me to come down here to be your counselor. I guess to give you something pretty to look at as well, but there's no amount of money in the world that'll turn me into *anyone's* sex slave. I'm not that woman, so please release those nasty thoughts from your head," she retorted sassily.

I think I'm in real love for the first time in forever. Donny thought to himself.

"That's my fault, right there. I came at you the wrong way. Let's start over... I'm Donny."

Malik D. Rice

Chapter 28

Jelissa made a surprise visit to the Young & Foolish center, in Fayette-ville, to see how things were running, when nobody knew she was coming.

Sheila was the building's manager. She oversaw everything that went on concerning the YF center. She was a middle-aged Black woman, that was struggling to keep her youth programs above float before Jelissa found her and made her dream come true. Now, she was a part of the biggest youth support system in the state of North Carolina.

"You know how much I love the youth, girl. They're the future, and so many of them are in danger of getting caught up in this screwed society, but this center gives them so much hope. I can see it in their eyes." Sheila ranted, as they took a slow stroll through the center.

All that could be heard was their heels clacking on the hard granite floor, and kids yelling in the background.

"I really like the way you're running things here, and the love that the kids have for you is amazing. I definitely commend you for..." Jelissa was cut short mid-sentence, when she spotted Nequa along with two other men, standing down the hall.

Nequa was already looking at her, with a smile, before Jelissa even noticed Nequa. Since she was already walking, she made her way over to Nequa, and her company. "Long time, no see. How long have you been back in the city? I heard you were gone for good," Jelissa mentioned after giving Nequa a warm hug.

"I've been out here for a lil' while now. I took over Donny's spot and what-not. How have you been? I have been hearing great things about you. I'm real proud of you and Manny," said Nequa.

"Thanks, but I've been very busy, trying to keep it all together. Sometimes I swear the government is deliberately trying to sabotage my mission, but I don't let it get to me... Who's your company?" She asked, referring to the two men, who stood silently behind Nequa.

Nequa turned to them, and back at Jelissa. "Oh, this is Blu and Cleezy. They wanted to see the center for themselves, so I'm just showing them. They plan on making a nice donation to the cause too."

"Cleezy... I remember that name." Jelissa admitted aloud while racking her brain, trying to remember where she knew him from.

"That's, Cleezy, from the west side," Nequa informed.

Jelissa's facial expression began to change, for the worse.

"Nah, it's not what you think. He's not with the Crip's no more. It's a long story, but he's YF now. Him, and all of his lil' homies." said Nequa.

"Wooooowww! I see there's been a lot going on out here... Anyway, welcome to the center and welcome to YF. Please make us look good because what y'all do in the streets reflects what I'm trying to do in the corporate world," Jelissa stated seriously.

Cleezy nodded his understanding, with an equally serious expression. "I'm witnessing, first-hand, everything that YF is offering the community. I really feel bad, that I haven't donated to the cause sooner, but now that I'm a part of the cause, and plan to do my part to the fullest... I'm promoting nothing, but peace, love, and prosperity. I just have one situation to handle first."

***

Dizzy hadn't stepped foot into Snake Wood since he found out about Nasty's demise. He was a wrecking ball the last time he'd been there, but now, he was more level-headed.

"I'm not gon' lie. You had the most to gain from Nasty's death, so you were the main suspect in my eyes, but now I know that you're innocent. I came here face-to-face to apologize, my nigga. You a good Demon, and you put in a lot of work for the hood. You deserve your spot, just as much as Nasty deserved his."

Dizzy was a standup nigga, so when he was wrong, he admitted it with no problem, and right now was a prime example. Crimson respected him for it. "It's all good, bruh. I know how much you fucked with Nasty. What happened though? How you find out? You know who did it? All you got to do is point the finger. Their ass is *grass*."

"Nahhhh, just chill for now. It'll be too easy to whack 'em. I'm trying to think of the proper torture for them." Dizzy informed evilly.

Crimson's face crumbled up. "Who the fuck is it? This suspense is killing me, bruh!"

"A Crip nigga from Cali named Falcon."

Malik D. Rice

Chapter 29

For security measures, Falcon boosted his personal security. There was too much going on, and the stakes were too high, for him to take any chances.

He was at the house, waiting for Tito to pull up. He needed to send the young nigga on a top-secret mission, to find out DG and YF's stash spots and trap spots, so they could burn all of that shit down. It would be the power move that would put a hole in their pockets.

"So, how we gon' play it? We gon' hit 'em with a series of attacks, how they did us that one night?" X asked as he joined Falcon on the back porch.

Falcon watched his new pit bull fumbling with a big bone, he'd bought out of Walmart. Little shit like this gave him peace in the midst of all the chaos around him.

"We gon' play the backfield until lil' Tito report back with some valuable information, then we gon' make our move. I don't want to shoot up any random corners, or spots. I want to do some real damage, and this is the best way." Falcon informed irritably. He was getting tired of the way X had been breathing down his back lately.

X sighed, and took a seat on the top step, next to Falcon. "Listen. I don't be trying to bother you, cuz. I just be asking you questions because the homies come to me asking questions that they're scared to ask you. We already against the odds, and it's starting to get some of them second-guessing. I just now got word that it was talk about some of the homies in the set thinking about going YF. Something's got to give."

Falcon turned towards his enforcer slowly with a nasty mug. "What? Who?"

"I don't even know yet, but I got..." X was cut short by booming thunderous sounds.

It only took a second for them to realize what it was. It was heavy gunfire.

Tat-tat-tat-tat! Boom! Boom! Tat-tat-tat-tat! Boom! Boom! Boc! Boc! Boc! Boc! Boc! Different kinds of guns went off in unison, and it sounded like a full-fledged war was going on out front.

X jumped down the stairs, and made his way around the house, as quick as his fat legs would allow. He had his .45 in hand, ready to let it rip, but the assault was over with by the time he made it to the front yard. It was a mess.

A handful of his soldiers had jumped in a truck to pursue the shooters, that were escaping down the street, and the other soldiers, that remained, were attending to the two that were wounded during the assault.

"Get them in the truck! We about to get them to a hospital!" X commanded urgently.

"Leave 'em! The ambulance gon' come to them. Go in the house, and get all the drugs and money, then put that in the truck," Falcon overrode X's orders firmly.

X turned back and faced Falcon. "Them bitch ass niggas just hit us hard. Nobody was supposed to know about this spot."

"But Tito did," Falcon added while handing his phone over to X.

X looked down at the phone's screen through squinted eyes. It was a text message from Tito's phone that had just been sent a few seconds ago. *We do it for, NASTY! DG*

***

Dizzy spotted Tadoe climbing into his car when he pulled up into his neighborhood. He needed to talk to Tadoe, so he stopped at the end of his driveway, so he would be blocked in.

Tadoe immediately hopped out of his car and made his way down the driveway. Dizzy hopped out of his car as well. "Wassup, Unc?"

"Don't 'Unc' me, lil' nigga. Persia told me about y'all lil' episode. And even though we not that close, I was still mad at you for some time. You ain't the one that made no promises to me, so I can't really be mad at you. But you not gon' stand right there and call me Unc. We're the furthest thing away from family. Now, tell me why you in front of my driveway, blocking me off," Tadoe demanded sternly.

Dizzy was taken aback by Tadoe's statement. He didn't think that Persia would have the balls to tell him herself, but she definitely showed him wrong. Considering the circumstances, he couldn't even feel any type of way towards, Tadoe, for speaking to him in that manner. "Like you said, we not that close, and pussy is pussy. I couldn't help myself, but if it makes you feel any better, she don't want shit to do with me no more."

"Yeah, I know that much. Now answer my question. What you want, Dizzy?"

"I got a few extra hundred thousand and I'm trying to see what you gon' charge me to wash it."

"Half," Tadoe answered through an evil smirk. It was time for payback.

Dizzy gave him a knowing look. "Really?"

"Take it or leave it. You really expect..." Tadoe was cut short by rapid gunfire.

Neither one of them had time to escape the oncoming bullets.

Malik D. Rice

Chapter 30

Leavenworth Prison was running smoothly for the first time in a long time, just as Donny promised. There was a structure in place, and disputes were being handled through politics, and not knives. The administration was pleased with the shift of energy and hoped that it lasted.

Donny wished that things were running as smoothly in Rondoville, as they were in Leavenworth. He was just on the phone with, Nequa. She filled him in on the tragic events that took place the night before.

Apparently, Falcon didn't take well to the little message that Dizzy sent his way, so he retaliated with two messages of his own.

He caught Dizzy down bad in front of Tadoe's house, and lit both of them up, leaving both of them laid up in bad shape, and he also had the YF center shot up badly. Nobody was there, but the janitor, but it was a critical moment for the city, and Donny felt like it was his mess to clean up. In a way, it basically was.

Knock! Knock! Knock!

"Come in!" He yelled at whoever was on the other side of his cell door.

One of the Mobsters who was on duty, doing security outside of his room, stuck his head in the door. "The booth officer just sent word that you got a visit."

"A legal visit?"

The Mobster shook his head *no*. "Hell nah. The twin already asked. It's a regular visit. I guess they got you on special visitation days too."

"Damn... Alright then. I'm about to get ready. Gather up ten Mobsters, y'all coming up there with me." He instructed before getting himself together.

The whole time he dressed, he couldn't help, but wonder who had come to visit him this time. He knew it wasn't Manny because he was scheduled to come on a later date, but Manny was unpredictable, so he really didn't know shit.

Donny already had on a pair of white and black Adidas jogging pants, so he just slid on a pair of all-white Air Force Ones, and a white Ralph Lauren V-neck shirt, along with all five of his chains and his watch.

He then gathered his ten Mobsters, grabbed the visitation pass from the booth officer, and headed up front to go feed his curiosity.

"I understand your status, and all, but did you really have to bring this much security to your own visitation?" A female guard asked Donny while scanning his body with a metal detector.

"Apparently, he doesn't go anywhere without them. You can't really blame him though. I probably would do the same if I were in his shoes," Mr. Ridge admitted, to Donny's surprise.

Donny nodded his head. "Yeah, I'll usually have at least twenty of them with me, but I cut it in half since y'all gave me my own visitation day."

It was a Friday, and visitation days were normally on Saturdays and Sundays, so Donny would have the entire visitation area to himself. Just how he'd arranged.

"Enjoy your visit, Donny." Mr. Ridged said after the female guard was done scanning all of the Mobsters with the portable wand.

Donny walked through the door, into the visitation area, and was surprised when he spotted Hennessey patiently waiting on him at a table, in the middle of the room.

He was very surprised to see her, but he kept his cool. He hadn't heard from her since the day before his sex tape was leaked and didn't think he'd be hearing from her any time soon. So many emotions were brewing inside of him, but he kept a lid on them as he calmly strolled her way.

"Y'all post up at these tables and wait on me," Donny commanded needlessly, but he just wanted to do some shit to mask his uneasiness.

He then locked eyes with Hennessey as he neared her. She didn't stand to greet or hug him, so he just took a seat and continued to stare at her. He'd been keeping up with her social media, so her growing belly was no surprise, and her pregnant glow wasn't either. She was more beautiful than she'd ever been.

"I hate to say I told you so, but I told you so. Look at you now. You're in prison with all this damn time over your head... *I told you* not to get taken out of the game. We were supposed to have a future together." said Hennessey with much hurt in her tone and eyes.

Donny knew she was right and felt bad that he'd let her down, but his pride wouldn't let it be known. "So, this what you came for? To state the fuckin' obvious? I called and texted you a thousand times since I got my cell phone, you could've told me then. I know I fucked up, but I don't deserve for my own baby mamma to turn her back on a nigga."

"Ughhh." She sighed audibly. "Actually, that's why I came. I respected you enough not to tell you this over the phone... I'm getting pretty serious with this movie director, and I've come to the conclusion that he'll make a more suitable father for my child, so if you ever loved me, you'll just let me be, and you'll let this baby be," she said while rubbing her, growing, stomach.

Donny couldn't help it. The mask was off because he couldn't hide the unmeasurable wave of pain that just washed over his soul. He never knew how much Hennessey actually meant to him until that exact second. He wanted to beg for her to stay, but his pride wouldn't dare let him begin to do it, so he did what he did best. Sucked the shit up.

"Say less, and I wish y'all the best." He lied with a straight face, before getting up, and walking off, while fighting the tears that threatened to fall.

Hennessey called after him, but he kept walking. The single tear that escaped his eye was a signal of their fallen bond. He knew deep down that they would *never* speak again. He would grant her wish because it turned out that he actually did love her all this time.

Malik D. Rice

Chapter 31

Persia cried on Sasha's shoulder in the hospital waiting area. She was broken and was literally falling into pieces. They sat with Tadoe's family, as they waited for the doctor to hurry back with some kind of news.

"It's *alllll* my fault, Sasha. Tadoe is laid up in that hospital bed all because of my stupid ass." Persia cried out.

"Girl, that's not true. That was just retaliation from some rivals. You didn't have nothing to do with that shit that happened today," Sasha assured comfortingly. She began looking around, trying to see if one of Tadoe's family members overheard Persia. Luckily, they didn't. She was just as broken as Persia about Tadoe getting shot, but she was being strong for her friend.

"They were in the driveway talking when they got shot at. Tadoe would've been gone already if he wasn't right there talking to Dizzy, and I know for a fact they were talking about me, so like I said, it's all my fault."

Sasha rubbed her head. "Just calm down, baby. Everything's going to be just fine, and Tadoe's going to make it."

***

Crimson had everything to gain at the moment. He was from the Evil Side and was the Top Demon in the hood, but even he wasn't evil enough to wish death on his homie, even if benefited him. If Dizzy were to die on that hospital bed, he would be the Don over their camp, but that's not what he wanted. He wanted Dizzy to live.

The other Demons in the hood were grim and wanted blood to avenge Dizzy, but he had to force them to sit their asses down. Shit was too hot in the city at the moment. The YF center was one of the most positive things to ever happen to Fayetteville, and nobody was happy about the building getting turned into a crime scene, especially not the police, because the public was blaming them.

Every move, from now on, had to be carefully calculated because the police were definitely waiting for someone to make the next move. So, he put revenge on the backburner and focused on his operation because business had to continue.

"We been doing businesses with these niggas in South Carolina for a while, but they been buying twelve pounds for the longest, now they trying to up the shipment to twenty-five, so y'all need to be on point because y'all know how the game goes. It might be a possible jack move, so if y'all peep *anything* off about them niggas, y'all got the greenlight to chop they asses down." He instructed a group of Demons, before tossing them a thick duffle bag.

He sat back down on the wooden table and proceeded to count his money, as they exited the basement. He was in his preferred place of business. It wasn't his house, it was just one of the rundown houses in the hood, that he chose to operate out of.

"Get yo' ass up, bitch!" He spat half-jokingly, at the pretty redbone he'd been fucking on, for the past few weeks. "You sitting there looking all pretty, and shit. You need to be helping me count this money."

She sucked her teeth and sighed heavily, but she got her ass up and grabbed a stack of the money.

"Matter-a-fact, go over there to the other table and bag them pounds up. That's 448 grams, and they better not be a gram off either... Fuck wrong with you?" he asked rhetorically. He was starting to get tired of her ass any damn way.

A heavy set of footsteps came down the stairs, causing him to grab his gun, and hop off the table alertly. He relaxed a little when Low-Low emerged. He was one of Crimson's Top Demons. "How the trip go?"

"Smooth as Denzell on a good day. Them Florida niggas always do good business," he informed, before handing Crimson a Prada shopping bag, filled with different bills.

Crimson peeped inside the bag and nodded his approval. "That's what I like to hear. We might have to drop the prices a lil' bit though, and get up off of this shit, because shit hot in the city, so we just gon' wholesale all this shit."

"That's cool. I'm definitely with it, but guess who I ran across on my way here after I got off the highway?"

"Who?" Crimson asked while looking up at him curiously. "You better not say my lil' sister because I'm gon' beat her lil' ass if she back fuckin' with that old head again."

"Nahhh, man... I ran into Lil' Dizzy walking on Bragg Boulevard by himself. At first, I didn't know who the hell he was because he had on a hoodie, but he just so happened to turn his head, and I had to swerve over two lanes just to pick his lil' ass up."

"Where he at?"

Low-Low nodded his head upwards. "Outside kicking it with the Demons."

"Go get him!"

A few minutes later, Lil' Dizzy came down the stairs to the basement by himself. "Wassup Crimson?"

"I should be asking you the same. Why the hell you walking down Bragg by yourself? If one of them Crip niggas would've snatched you up, then what?" Crimson's stomach churned just at the thought. "Yo' daddy would've gone on a rampage."

"Them crackers tried to come in the house and pick me up after the spot got shop up. I damn sure wasn't about to go to no group home, so I slid out the back. I was making my way to the hood when Low-Low picked me up. I just had to stop by one of my friend's house for a while because that's a long-ass walk, and I was hungry."

Crimson looked at the lil' nigga and seen so much of his father inside of him. He was a literal reflection. Even at his young age, he carried himself like a young boss. "At least you know your own way around the city... I'm just glad Low-Low spotted you when he did."

Lil' Dizzy waved him off. "Fuck all that, man. I'm ready to catch my first body," he informed, before pulling out the .25 Dizzy gave him for emergencies.

Crimson slapped his face and shook his head.

Malik D. Rice

Chapter 32

"Hey, Deanna. How you doing?" Rondo asked, through the phone.

"Hey, Rondo... I'm doing just fine, now that your cousin is in my life. He just doesn't know how much of a blessing he is," she admitted truthfully.

Jay leaned over and kissed her on the lips. "Let me take this call outside, bae."

He got up and walked out of the RV. He knew Rondo wanted to talk business, and Deanna didn't need to be a part of it. She already knew way more than she was supposed to, and he wasn't going to worry her with his current dilemmas.

"I know, I know. Shit went left field real quick. Nobody expected for that nigga, Falcon, to be such a problem. Especially after Cleezy went YF, but you know what they say about wild animals."

"What they say about wild animals, Jay?" Rondo asked, knowing there were a lot of sayings about wild animals.

"Them muthafuckas will lash out when they feel like they're cornered, and Falcon ain't no different. That nigga snapped when he shot up the YF building. It's gon' draw a lot of unwanted attention." said Jay.

"Mmm-hmmm! I'm glad you evaluated the entire situation. Now, you can start formulating a plan to fix it before shit gets out of hand. You and Donny better put y'all heads together," Rondo spat, before ending the call.

"Ughhhhhh!" Jay sighed, as he slid his phone back into his back pocket.

Normally, he would've been amped up, and ready to hop into action, but things were different now. The quiet life was starting to grow on him, and Deanna was definitely growing on him. He'd much rather sit up in the house with her than to run the streets, but duty was calling, and he had to answer.

"Everything okay?" Deanna asked as he walked back inside.

He walked over to her and sat down on the couch next to her. "Yeah, but I'm about to have to leave for a couple of days."

"Take me with you!" she insisted in a pouty manner with her lip poked out.

He looked at her knowingly, even though he knew she couldn't see him. "Now, you know damn well you can't go with me, shawty. I love spending time with you, and I wish you could take you with me, but you know why you can't."

"I'm just messing with you, baby," she informed jokingly. "but I'm going to need you to be safe. Do what you need to do and come back to me please."

Jay looked at his woman and smiled inwardly. Never in a million years did he ever think he'd end up falling in love with a blind woman, but he was highly thankful that God linked them two together. She completed him and gave him an extra sense of purpose. "Oh, you ain't got to worry about that. I'm definitely coming home to your lil' sexy ass. Now give me some more kisses before I go!"

He basically jumped on top of her and started raining sloppy kisses all over her face, while tickling the sides of her stomach and making her laugh in blissful pleasure.

***

Falcon took over an entire motel on the north side. He bought every room in the building and gained a clear understanding with the owner. It was a move he was forced to make, but he wasn't complaining. War came with unfortunate situations. He was determined to come out on top though.

He was in his room, sitting on the bed, taking long drags from a Newport 100. He struggled to come up with his next plan.

His drug operation was on hold since he only delt locally. He had money saved up, so he wasn't tripping, but he was losing soldiers by the day. More and more of his soldiers were gravitating over to Cleezy since he was favored to win the war between the two, and nobody liked to be on the losing side.

It had got to a point where Falcon said fuck it and abandoned the Crips in Fayetteville. They would end up running to Cleezy anyway, so he only moved into the motel with his soldiers that came from Cali with him.

He was determined, but he wasn't stupid. He knew the war for Fayetteville was a lost cause. The city belonged to DG and YF now. Anyone could see that. He'd recently made peace with the fact, but there was still one more thing that needed to be done before he retreated back to California.

Cleezy had to go.

***

Tadoe got shot in his back twice and another bullet grazed his neck. He was in a world of pain, but he was still alive, and he was blessed for that.

He was reflecting on his life, when Persia walked into his room, looking like the young goddess that he continued to see her be. "I would tell you to come to hop on this dick, but I'm scared I might paralyze myself trying to catch a nut," he joked harshly.

"That's not funny at all, baby!" she spat seriously after taking a seat in the chair beside his bed. "Don't say nothing about being paralyzed. That shit scares the fuck out of me."

"I'm saying, what if I was to get paralyzed? Would you still be here?" he asked seriously, after turning his head to the side so he could see her.

She stared at him blankly for a short while. "That's not a fair question, Tadoe, and you know it."

"Exactly. Get up out of here, man... Let me get some sleep because you just making shit worse right about now," he spat harshly, before turning his head to the opposites side of the room.

She stood up and looked down at him sadly. She wanted to say something to him so badly, but decided that it'd be wise to let him be for now. He was in a lot of pain, under a lot of stress, and obviously not in his correct state of mind.

She bent down, gave him a soft kiss on his exposed neck, and exited the room quietly.

A few minutes later, Persia finessed her way past Dizzy's security at his door and walked into his room.

Dizzy was sound asleep on the hospital bed, and he looked highly uncomfortable. He took two bullets to the torso and one to the midsection. He was in very bad shape.

Persia walked up to the bed and peered down at him for a long while. One of the bullets must've hit something important because he had a breathing tube wedged into his mouth and he also looked frail.

He must've sensed her energy or something because his eyes popped open. He was alert and paranoid until he noticed it was Persia. He relaxed instantly, and let it show in his eyes. He honestly didn't think he would make it and was glad that someone was there to check on him. It warmed his cold heart a little bit.

"I blame you for what happened to Tadoe, and I pray that you die on this hospital bed!" Persia informed harshly before hawking up mucus from her chest and spit a nasty glob of mushy saliva in his face.

The little bit of warmth that Dizzy allowed in his heart was gone again, just that fast. He watched as she stormed out of the room and wasn't even upset with her for what she'd just done or said. He was in so much pain physically, and dull internally. He felt helpless and hopeless as the spit slid down the side of his face.

Persia exited his mind just as fast as she exited the room. His mind shifted to Venom. His archenemy. He thought back on all the times that Venom had to lay up in a hospital bed, and how he must've felt. He came back strong *every time*, and Dizzy had gained a new respect for Venom. He was a strong muthafucka, to take all the shit that life threw at him, and still carry on like it wasn't shit.

As much as he hated Venom, right then, the nigga was his biggest inspiration and motivation. He would make it out of that hospital bed, and he would live to be there for his son.

Chapter 33

Jay popped up in Snake Wood with no care in the world. It was definitely the most dangerous neighborhood in the city and niggas knew not to pull up uninvited, but he figured that they wouldn't shoot at a nigga on a motorcycle. They'd be more curious to see who it was.

He only came to Snake Wood once, and that's when Rondo popped up on Dizzy a while ago. It was different last time because Rondo was running the show. He was his own boss now and saw things from a different light. He had to make his own decisions and had to make sure they were the right decisions.

He approached a corner where a handful of young niggas posted up at and chose to stop there. He parked the bike and took his helmet off so they could see who he was. They obviously didn't recognize him because they began to approach him with their weapons drawn.

He got off the bike, and rested the helmet on the seat, before turning towards them with his hands in the air. "Listen, this ain't what y'all lil' niggas want. Y'all obviously don't know my face, but I'm sure y'all done heard the name. I'm DG Jay."

Like he expected, they lowered their weapons at the mention of his name. "Why you ain't just say nothing big bruh? You know how it goes down out here. We don't tolerate outsiders. What's up though? You got to be looking for Crimson because Dizzy laid up in the hospital." One of the young Demons responded.

Jay nodded his head, and they took him to Crimson.

***

The sun was setting, and Crimson was finally winding down for the evening. He'd been up since four o'clock in the morning, handling business with no rest. He chose to take the rest of the night off to relax before he had to do it all over again the next day. The Demons would keep shit afloat until he emerged.

He had just plopped on the couch with a fat ass bowl of cereal when he heard the doorbell ring. "Damn, mannn! A nigga can't even get a few hours to himself these days," he complained, but he still went to answer the door.

It could've been anyone, and he was right. He looked through the peephole and spotted, Jay. He remembered the young boss; from the last time, he came with Rondo.

He quickly opened the door. "Jay. Wassup bruh?"

Jay didn't respond immediately, he walked past, Crimson, into the house. He took a seat on the couch, grabbed Crimson's bowl of cereal, and started eating it, with his feet up on the table.

Crimson walked into the living room behind him, with a very unpleasant face. "You comfortable enough? You want me to roll you up a blunt too, nigga?" he asked sarcastically.

Jay shook his head. "Nah, I don't even smoke no more, but what you can do is put that nigga Falcon, in the dirt. In here laid up and eating cereal in a robe. Fuck is wrong with you, nigga?"

"I just got in bruh. Plus, it's too hot in the streets, right now, to make a move. That's exactly what the police waiting on."

Jay stood up and walked up to Crimson. "Like I said, find out a way to get the muthafuckin' job done, or Snake Wood gon' be lookin' for a new Top Demon," he threatened, then let himself out just how he let himself in.

Chapter 34

All around the city the police were applying pressure. They were raiding drug spots and making arrests by the boatloads. The Mayor made them feel it for the YF center shooting, so they were making the streets feel it.

"Okay. What that got to do with me? Donny not trying to hear that shit. He wants his money paid on time, regardless of the situation. Y'all niggas been doing this shit for a long time, and y'all know exactly how this shit work... If the police went into y'all spot and took all the drugs, then y'all need to be breaking into their spot and taking the drugs back or pay them dues out y'all pockets. I don't give a fuck how y'all get it, just make sure I get mines, or y'all asses gon' end up on the skillet," Nequa spat coldly. She fucked with Trappa and Rod, but she wouldn't let anybody fuck her money up, or her face-card.

Trappa nodded his head, but Rod sucked his teeth.

"Got something you want to say, Rod? Keep playing with me, and I'll have yo ass dropped down to a Mobster nigga. Think this shit a game if you want. Yeah, I'm a bitch, but y'all niggas know I can get *real* niggaish if I need to," Nequa reminded, looking at them through piercing eyes.

"Nah, you got it. We'll get the money." Rod promised, before leaving her house before he ended up saying something that would complicate his situation further. It took an enormous amount of pride to do that.

When he was gone, Trappa, spoke. "We gon' come up with the money. We weren't expecting them to hit the stash spot."

"Make sure you do that because I got too much on my plate as it is. Donny locked up, but he more powerful as ever because he using them politics to his advantage, and I'm not trying to end up on the wrong side of those politics."

Trappa nodded, before standing. "I got you, sis'. Everything gon' get handled on time."

***

Lil Dizzy was getting restless and begging to catch a body in his father's name. Of course, Crimson wasn't going to allow that to happen on his watch, but he did have to do something to ease the young niggas mind, and what better way to do that, than to take him to visit Big Dizzy.

They walked into the room and found Dizzy laying on the bed. "See, I told you he not dying. You hear that monitor beeping. That's his heartbeat. He still kicking, and gon' keep kicking. Your dad is one of the toughest niggas I know," Crimson assured.

Lil' Dizzy ran over to the bed and looked at his father through intense eyes. "What's the shit in his mouth? Why his eyes not open?"

"That's a tube to help him breathe correctly, and the doctors got him on some strong medicine to help him sleep through the pain, so he just sleeping good, that's all."

Lil' Dizzy shook his head with his teeth clenched. It hurt him to see his superhero looking like this. He grabbed his feather's hand, as a single tear fell down his face. He tried his best to be strong, and hold the river back, but it was to no avail. He broke down sobbing like the kid he was.

It hurt, Crimson, to see his young nigga broken like that. Looking at Lil' Dizzy carry on, he started to regret the decision of bringing him to the hospital. He should've at least waited for Dizzy to be able to talk to his son.

He bent down, scooped Lil' Dizzy up, and left out of the room.

"I got $50,000 for Falcon's life and $25,000 for his location... I'm sure one of y'all niggas can find out something. He somewhere out here on the north side. Y'all niggas traded when Cleezy and I needed y'all the most, but it's all good. Falcon from the Motherland, and probably made y'all all kinds of promises, but his ass is a dead man and YF is the future, so now, you either get with this shit or get rolled over. Anybody standing out here that still wants to rock a blue flag?"

Blu looked around at all the lieutenants of the north side, and none of them said a word, meaning they were all on board. "Good. As of right now, I'm welcoming the north side to join the YF community." He went on, breaking down the importance of the structure to them, and the zero-tolerance policy.

As of right then, the entire city belonged to DG and YF. It was set in stone, and there was *nobody* that could stop their reign.

Malik D. Rice

Chapter 35

Donny was working out with a large group of his Mobsters, when another one of his Mobsters called his name, from the booth. "Yooo, Donny! They just said to get dressed for yo' visit. Manny waiting for you up front!"

The whole dorm got quiet for a second, then they started cheering, ranting, and raving in excitement like they were the ones who were going to see Manny.

Donny smiled, shook his head, and jogged to his room to get his things ready for the shower. He rushed to get ready for his visit because he didn't want to keep Manny waiting too long.

"Woooooo! Look at my muthafuckin' brudda, man! You in this bitch lookin' like a million dollars cash, nigga! That's what the fuck I'm talking about!" Manny spat animatedly, as Donny walked into the visitation area, with ten lucky Monsters behind him.

"Wassup lil' nigga? You lookin' good too bruh. I missed yo' ass man. Tell me something good." Donny stated, after embracing his comrade.

They both sat down at the table.

"Just been living my life to the fullest, bruh. I figure the better I am, the better off mines are, and that's including you... My sons have been asking about you too."

That brought a smile to Donny's face. "Tell them lil' niggas I said wassup. How is Jelissa doing?"

"That's a real boss bitch, right there. She's been handling *all* the business. Like, it's to the point where I don't gots to do nothing but worry about my career because she's literally handling the rest, and I praise her for it."

"That's the type of shit I like to hear. What you working on now?"

Manny gave him a knowing look. "You know I'm working on that *Free Donny* album."

"Nooooo! You ain't tell me that, bruh. An album? Sheesh! That's major, right there." Donny was genuinely touched.

Manny waved him off. "You deserve it, fool... Anyway, wassup with you though? I know you doing good time in here, but you're still locked up with all this time, and it has to be affecting you in some type of way."

"Of course, it is. But you know I'm a solid nigga, so I ain't easily broken. For the most part, I learned a lot about the system, other people, and most importantly myself. It's a double-edged sword, I guess."

"At least you using all this time to broaden your horizon and analyze certain things. You been reading books in here?"

Donny nodded his head *yes.* "Yeah, but not novels. I have been ordering self-help books and mostly psychological books. Every great leader needs to master the human mind in order to manipulate their followers."

"Damn, that's cold," Manny responded quickly.

Donny shook his head in disagreement. "There are two sides to everyone and everything. When people hear the word *manipulation,* they automatically go to thinking negative, but they look past the fact that people can actually be manipulated into doing the right thing."

"Damn. I can't even argue with that because it's some real shit... I'm not gon' lie, a lot of people are disappointed in you, but not me. I'm proud of you, my nigga. In a weird way, I believe this prison shit is gon' end up being the best thing to ever happen to you. You gon' do great things with that mind of yours. I always knew you were smarter than you let yourself be." Manny admitted warmly.

At first, Donny's face crumpled up, but he had to shift his perception. He understood where Manny was coming from. "I should start writing books like that nigga, Santana, huh? He locked up, but he still making his voice heard and he putting on for this gang shit."

"I mean, your voice gon' be heard through me regardless, but I can understand you wanting folks to hear from you personally. If you feel like you can do it, do it bruh. I'm behind you no matter what. I'm just glad you not letting these walls close in on you."

"Definitely not. I mean, I got discouraged when I found out about Hennessey, but I started thinking about that counselor you sent down here and got right." Donny informed jokingly.

Manny smirked back at him evilly. "Yeahhhhh! That's a bad bitch, huh? I knew they was gon' hire her on the spot. She's here for you. What you do wit' her, is on you though."

"She is sophisticated, smart, and beautiful as hell. I'm trying to marry that bitch," Donny joked seriously.

Manny laughed at the statement, then his smile slowly faded. "I heard about that shit that happened at the YF center. Jelissa almost had a heart attack, bruh. Now we got to hire security for the center just so kids will feel safe coming there. It's supposed to be a safe haven, Donny. Wassup with that?"

"Yeah. I know, I know." Although Donny was locked up, he was still the Capo over Rondoville, so it was still his problem to resolve. "I know shit looks out of control right now, but it's not as complicated as you think. There's only one problem and that muthafucka about to get solved *real soon*... I got Jay on the job, and you know that nigga gon' get every job done by any means."

Manny nodded his agreement. "YF."

"To death!" Donny retorted firmly.

Malik D. Rice

Chapter 36

Blu went to Nequa's house to check up on her. They'd been spending a lot of time together lately and were surely growing on each other.

She vented to him about her recently growing stress, and her desire to get back out of the game, to live a simpler life. Blu felt her situation, and he also felt for her.

It must've shown in his eyes, as he sat there staring at her, as she spoke. "Why are you looking at me like that?" She asked uneasily. She couldn't remember the last time a man looked at her like that.

He didn't even answer, he just leaned over and kissed her intensely. Everything about her turned him on, and he couldn't help himself. She didn't resist his advances, so he leaned her back on the couch until she laid on her back, looking up at him with wide eyes.

Blu took off his shirt, and tossed it across the living room, before removing the PINK sweatpants she wore, with ease. To his surprise, she didn't have on any panties underneath, and her pretty phat pink pussy was exposed after he pulled off her PINK pants. "Damn!" He said before biting his lip seductively.

"What?" She asked, now looking up at him insecurely.

"Nothing. I didn't know your pussy was so pretty. That's all," he informed, while gently massaging it with his right hand. She was becoming moister by the second.

"You gon' give her a kiss like you just gave me?"

He shifted himself down on the couch and showed her better than he could tell her. He literally dug his face in between her legs and got in there. He ate her pussy like it was crack candy. Slurping, licking, and sucking on her clit.

"Oh! Oh! Shittt!" she cried in pleasure, while squeezing his head with both hands, and her eyes shut tightly.

He reached up and slipped his hands under her shirt, so he could feel on her big titties with one hand and jacked himself off with the other.

They both were in paradise, but if someone were watching them, they probably would laugh because of the awkward way they were positioned. Definitely two squirrels trying to get a nut.

The Devil had to be real because right when Nequa was starting to feel an orgasm come along, her phone wanted to ring. "God damnnnnn!" she spat unpleasantly.

"Fuck it. You can call 'em back," Blu encouraged, looking up at her with her juices all over his face. It looked like he'd just stuck his face in a watermelon.

Nequa was tempted, but there was too much going on for her to be missing calls right now. "Hold on, baby. I got to get it." She slid her sweatpants back on and walked over to the kitchen counter to grab her phone.

"Yeah?" she answered the phone irritably.

It was, Trappa, and he requested to meet her as soon as possible. She knew that he knew better than to say too much over the phone, but she could tell from the urgency in his voice, that she needed to get there.

"I'm on my way," she informed before ending the call and grabbing her truck keys off the counter.

"You can stay here, or you can leave and come back another time, but I have to go handle this business now," she said to Blu.

Blu found his shirt and put it on. "Nah, I'd rather go with you." He saw the ounce of concern in her face and had the urge to ensure her safety.

"Well, bring your sexy ass on then. I got to go," she flirted seriously before leading the way out of the house.

Trappa told Nequa to meet him at his house. When she pulled up, he was waiting outside on his steps, smoking a cigarette. When he saw them pull up into his driveway, he walked into the house, leaving the front door open.

"That's some suspect ass shit he just did," Blu acknowledged while taking his pistol off safety.

"Nah, you don't have to worry about him. He and I got history like a muthafucka. He would never cross me," she assured after turning the car off and putting the keys in her purse.

Blu looked over at her and raise a curious brow.

"And *no*! It's not even like that. He's really like a brother to me, that's all."

"Aight, cool. I believe you. Let's go see what he wants then." Said Blu, before opening his door and stepping out of the car.

Nequa did the same, but she was smiling inwardly because of the way Blu just called himself getting jealous over her. She could definitely get used to that.

"Trap! Where you at, bruh!" Nequa called out, upon them entering the house.

"In the kitchen, sis'!" Trappa answered.

Nequa led the way to the kitchen, and they caught Trappa pouring dog food into his bulldog's bowl.

"You ain't gon' believe the shit I just heard."

"What?" Nequa asked urgently. She'd been waiting all this time to find out what was going on, and she was getting restless.

"I was on the phone talking strategy with this nigga, Rod, right."

Nequa nodded her understanding, and for him to continue.

"When it was time to hang up the phone, I guess he thought he hung up, but he didn't. I was pre-rolling my blunts, so I had the phone on speaker when it sounded like I heard a car door shut. I went to call his name, but I guess he didn't have me on speaker, so he couldn't hear me. I was just about to hang up until I heard him say something about some money."

Nequa's face crumbled up now. "And then what?"

Trappa stood up with a sad look on his face. "That nigga the fuckin' police, man. He the reason the stash spot got hit. He sent the police at the stash spot, and they split the shit with him. I heard it *all*."

"I *knew* it was something fishy about that. Ain't nobody else know about the spot. How the hell the police end up raiding a spot that didn't have no traffic?"

Trappa nodded. "Yeah, man. I thought about the same shit, but I just chalked it up as a coincidence because I would've never thought he would do no snake shit like that."

"Me neither. That shit hurt a bitch, but I promise he gon' feel some pain too."

Chapter 37

Rod was in his bedroom counting money with his wife. She was so used to this process, she didn't even bother to complain about it anymore. He would let his daughter help him, but she had sticky fingers, and he didn't have time for it today.

"At this rate, we gon' be able to disappear real soon, baby. Like, another month type shit."

His wife stopped counting and looked up at him with wide eyes and an open mouth. "A month? Don't play with my emotions, Rod. We done been here before. Too many damn times!"

"Yeah, I know. I promised you a lot of shit before, but this shit is real. I'm tired of this shit. It's time for me to leave this shit behind," he vented seriously.

"Where did this come from? Nequa gave you the green light?" she asked excitedly.

He waved her off arrogantly. "Fuck Nequa baby. I got this, and I got us."

"Awwwww! I can't wait, baby. I got to start getting our shit ready!" she shouted, before throwing the money down and hopping on top of him.

They wrestled to get their clothes off, preparing to have hot sex on top of the bed full of money. It wasn't their first time doing it, but it didn't make the experience any less exciting.

Rod was flicking his tongue across her nipple when he heard his front door being kicked down. "Oh, shit!" he spat while rolling over, trying to make it to his gun on the dresser.

Boc! Nequa put a bullet in his back, stopping him short.

Rod's wife was on the floor curled up in a fetal position, screaming like somebody was raping her. "Shut the fuck up!" Trappa spat, after pulling a sock off of Rod's feet and stuffing it in her mouth. "We not here to hurt you, but if you move that sock, I'm gon' put a bullet there instead." He tone was deathly.

Nequa walked up on, Rod, who was groaning in pain while lying on his stomach helplessly. "You deserve every bit of this shit."

Rod didn't say anything. There was no need in pleading for his life or none of that sucker shit. He'd rolled the dice and crapped out. That's just the way it went. He didn't even want to know how they found out about his deceit because it didn't matter. He tried to outsmart the game, and it spanked him. He turned his head and looked down at his wife. He wanted her to be the last thing that he saw in this life.

Nequa raised her pistol, preparing herself to take Rod's life, but Blu stopped her by gently pushing her arm down. "Let me handle it, baby. You don't got to do this."

She laughed and raised her arm back up.

Boc! Boc! Boc! Boc!

Three bullets hit Rod in the back, and one hit him in the neck. He was definitely down for the count, and some.

"That's not my first body, hunny. I'm not your average bitch, I do this shit for real," she informed matter-of-factly with a smile. She planted a firm kiss on his lips and walked away, laughing at the situation.

Blu looked at Trappa once she was gone. Trappa shrugged his shoulders. "You got your hands full. That's a lot of woman rite there!"

"I see... I think I'm in love," Blu joked seriously before following behind her while Trappa quickly gathered all the money in the room.

***

It was midnight, but X still knocked on Falcon's motel door, and patiently waited for him to open it. He'd obviously just woke up out of his sleep, but X obviously didn't give a damn about that because he barged past Falcon and walked into the room.

"Oh, this shit better be good, nigga. I was just dreaming about Lauren London." Falcon informed seriously. Anybody, who knew him, knew that he didn't play when it came to Lauren.

"That's the problem. While you in here having wet dreams, and shit, the rest of us is sitting around getting anxious, wondering what our next move is going to be."

Falcon sat down, on his bed, and looked up at X. "Y'all don't need to be worried about our next move. Y'all just need to be ready to make it when I call it."

"That's the thing! When? We have been holed up in this damn motel for about a week now. We need to finish shit as quickly as possible, so we can get up out of here. It ain't safe for us in Fayetteville."

Falcon looked up at, X with a big smirk. "Life is real funny because when I first met you, you were one of the hardest niggas that I knew. Now, it's like you turning into a bitch."

Knock. Knock. Knock. Three soft knocks came on the door.

X breathed a breath of relief. That had to be God because he was *this close* to spazzing out on Falcon's ass.

Falcon got up and answered the door. At first, he couldn't see anybody, until he caught something from his peripheral vision, that made him look down. It was a skinny little kid. "What's up lil' man? You lost? Where yo' mamma at?"

"My mamma probably somewhere sucking dick for some coke," the youngin informed, with a straight face.

Falcon and X started laughing. They were both intrigued and amused by the young nigga with a potty mouth.

"What about yo' daddy? Somebody about to have to come get you because you can't be out here by yourself like this," Falcon stated.

The little boy dropped his head to the ground. "My daddy got shot not too long ago. He in the hospital right now."

Falcon looked back at X, who just shrugged his shoulders, then looked back down, but the young nigga was gone. He stuck his head out of the room and came face-to-face with the muzzle of Jay's 9mm.

Psst! He put one suppressed hollow tip bullet into Falcon's skull, ending his reign just that quickly.

He leaned into the room and popped X's big ass twice in the stomach before taking off jogging back to Crimson's car across the street from the motel where Lil' Dizzy and Crimson waited on him.

"*Please* tell me you whacked that bitch ass nigga!" Lil Dizzy ranted from the backseat once Jay hopped into the passenger's seat.

Crimson sped off into traffic quickly.

"Handled that business just like yo' pops would've," Jay informed, before reaching back and running a hand in Lil' Dizzy's nappy head.

All three of them were relieved. It was a victorious mission completed, and they had Lil' Dizzy to thank for it because they probably wouldn't have been able to pull it off without him. Dizzy was going to be proud of his son for what he'd done for the team.

Chapter 38

Rondo stepped off of the jet on Dinero's airstrip, and to his surprise, Dinero was waiting for him personally this time. "I see you done hustled your way into some of that Infinity."

"What? I don't know what you talking about. Never heard of it." He lied, with a straight face.

Dinero patted him on the back, with a knowing smirk. "Yeah, I know that's right... I like that new spot you got. Real low-key."

Rondo stopped walking. "How you know? You saw my house."

"I got the all-seeing-eye, shawty. I know *everything* about mines. I had the spot scoped out before you even moved in." Dinero admitted seriously.

Rondo shook his head disappointedly and continued walking up the path. "You need to stop yo' shit, man. What, you don't trust a nigga?"

"Nah, it ain't that. I just feel the need to know everything about mines. Especially those in my secret society."

Rondo took a deep breath. "So, what you drag me up out of my cave for?"

"I want to show you something," Dinero informed, before hopping in a tricked-out golf cart.

Rondo hopped into the passenger seat, and Dinero drove off.

Five minutes later, they were pulling up to a warehouse on the far side of Dinero's estate.

"This where I keep all the motorbikes and all kinds of equipment," Dinero informed after hopping off of the cart.

Rondo hopped off of the cart. "I paid $2,500 for these shoes. I'm not about to ride no dirt bike in these, bro'."

"Man, bring yo' ass on," Dinero commanded.

They walked into the warehouse, and as Dinero said, there was an ass of motorbikes parked inside, along with rows of equipment to fix and build them. It was like a BMX rider's dream.

"This nice, but you ain't have to drag me all the way out here to see this shit, my nigga. You could've just sent a video or some pictures."

Dinero turned around and looked at Rondo with a straight face. "Rondo, shut the hell up and follow me."

Rondo wanted to carry on, but Dinero obviously had something more to show him, so he just followed his superior through the warehouse, until they reached the back.

"Watch this shit," Dinero said excitedly before opening up a door and leading the way down three flights of stairs.

They ended up on a lower level that looked sort of like a boiler room, but there was an elevator down there as well with shiny chrome doors. It looked totally out of place.

Dinero pressed the only button on the console, which was a down button, and turned around. Rondo stared at him curiously, but he didn't say anything. His curiosity would be craved soon enough.

A few moments later, the chrome doors opened, and they stepped onto the stylish elevator. It smelled like a new car, and DG Rell's lyrics played through the speakers.

Rondo stared at Dinero in amusement, as he bobbed his head playfully to the music. It brought a slight smile to his face because before he met Dinero, he would've bet his bottom dollar that the niggas was more soulless than Hitler, but he couldn't have been more wrong. Dinero was full of life still, and Rondo admired that about him.

The doors to the elevator opened, and Rondo couldn't believe his eyes. He stepped off of the elevator, and it opened up into a whole underground facility.

"Dilluminati Correctional Facility," Rondo read the large sign, that hung above the front desk. "What the fuck is this?"

"You just read the sign, nigga. It's a prison. A prison for made men in Dilluminati through. D.C.I."

Rondo stared at Dinero blankly. "Oh, you done lost yo' damn mind for real. You done made a prison for your *own* people?"

"Yeah. Four dorms with twenty cells apiece." He started walking further into the facility. "Made-men are the leaders of this organization. Everybody looks up to them, but unfortunately, very few have what it takes to claim the title, and that's what's wrong with Dilluminati now. Too many irreplaceable made men are getting whacked, sent to prison, or banned from their cities, so this is the solution."

Rondo nodded. "So, you're going to use this as another form of punishment for them?"

"Exactly. I made this prison for the same reason you made that bank in Rondoville. I created my own society, so it only makes sense to have all the necessary functions. And just like in the real world, prison is necessary... But it'll be just as much for their benefit, as it is for their punishment. They'll learn more about the world, and themselves. When they get finished with their sentence, they'll be released back onto their thrones, and they'll be more advanced, and more capable of leading, and teaching, their Mobsters a better way," Dinero sounded so passionate as he spoke.

"What about staff? Who's going to run the place?" Rondo asked curiously.

"I got nearly a hundred security guards at my deposal. I'll handpick about twenty of them and rotate them five at a time."

Rondo chuckled suddenly while shaking his head from side to side.

"What?" said Dinero.

"Yo' ass got too much time on your hands" Rondo joked seriously.

Dinero made a knowing face. "Look who's talkin'! This coming from the same man that's spending *all* that damn time holed up in an underground mansion. What are you and Alfred working on down there, Bruce Wayne?"

"Just chilllllll!" Rondo retorted playfully.

"Exactly, nigga... *We* got too much time on our hands, but we use it for the betterment of Dilluminati's future and that's all that matters. I changed the meaning to *Descendants of God* for a reason. That's how the oncoming generations are gon' feel about us," Dinero admitted before giving Rondo a better look at the place.

THE END... FOR NOW!!!

Submission Guideline

Submit the first three chapters of your completed manuscript to ldpsub-missions@gmail.com, subject line: Your book's title. The manuscript must be in a .doc file and sent as an attachment. Document should be in Times New Roman, double spaced and in size 12 font. Also, provide your synopsis and full contact information. If sending multiple submissions, they must each be in a separate email.

Have a story but no way to send it electronically? You can still submit to LDP/Ca$h Presents. Send in the first three chapters, written or typed, of your completed manuscript to:

LDP: Submissions Dept
Po Box 944
Stockbridge, Ga 30281

DO NOT send original manuscript. Must be a duplicate.

Provide your synopsis and a cover letter containing your full contact information.

Thanks for considering LDP and Ca$h Presents.

BOW DOWN TO MY GANGSTA

By **Ca$h**

TORN BETWEEN TWO

By **Coffee**

THE STREETS STAINED MY SOUL **II**

By **Marcellus Allen**

BLOOD OF A BOSS **VI**

SHADOWS OF THE GAME II

TRAP BASTARD II

By **Askari**

LOYAL TO THE GAME **IV**

By **T.J. & Jelissa**

IF LOVING YOU IS WRONG… **III**

By **Jelissa**

TRUE SAVAGE **VIII**

MIDNIGHT CARTEL IV

DOPE BOY MAGIC IV

CITY OF KINGZ III

By **Chris Green**

BLAST FOR ME **III**

A SAVAGE DOPEBOY III

CUTTHROAT MAFIA III

DUFFLE BAG CARTEL VI

HEARTLESS GOON VI

By **Ghost**

A HUSTLER'S DECEIT III

KILL ZONE **II**

BAE BELONGS TO ME III

A DOPE BOY'S QUEEN III

By **Aryanna**

COKE KINGS V

KING OF THE TRAP III

By **T.J. Edwards**

GORILLAZ IN THE BAY V

3X KRAZY III

De'Kari

THE STREETS ARE CALLING II

Duquie Wilson

KINGPIN KILLAZ IV

STREET KINGS III

PAID IN BLOOD III

CARTEL KILLAZ IV

DOPE GODS III

Hood Rich

SINS OF A HUSTLA II

ASAD

KINGZ OF THE GAME VI

Playa Ray

SLAUGHTER GANG IV

RUTHLESS HEART IV

By Willie Slaughter

FUK SHYT II

By Blakk Diamond

TRAP QUEEN

RICH $AVAGE II

By Troublesome

YAYO V

GHOST MOB II

Stilloan Robinson

CREAM III

By Yolanda Moore

SON OF A DOPE FIEND III

HEAVEN GOT A GHETTO II

By Renta

FOREVER GANGSTA II

GLOCKS ON SATIN SHEETS III

By Adrian Dulan

LOYALTY AIN'T PROMISED III

By Keith Williams

THE PRICE YOU PAY FOR LOVE III

By Destiny Skai

I'M NOTHING WITHOUT HIS LOVE II

SINS OF A THUG II

TO THE THUG I LOVED BEFORE II

By Monet Dragun

LIFE OF A SAVAGE IV

MURDA SEASON IV

GANGLAND CARTEL IV

CHI'RAQ GANGSTAS IV

KILLERS ON ELM STREET III

JACK BOYZ N DA BRONX II

A DOPEBOY'S DREAM II

By **Romell Tukes**

QUIET MONEY IV

Malik D. Rice

EXTENDED CLIP III

THUG LIFE IV

By **Trai'Quan**

THE STREETS MADE ME III

By **Larry D. Wright**

IF YOU CROSS ME ONCE II

ANGEL III

By **Anthony Fields**

FRIEND OR FOE III

By **Mimi**

SAVAGE STORMS III

By **Meesha**

BLOOD ON THE MONEY III

By J-Blunt

THE STREETS WILL NEVER CLOSE II

By K'ajji

NIGHTMARES OF A HUSTLA III

By King Dream

IN THE ARM OF HIS BOSS

By Jamila

CONCRETE KILLAZ II

By Kingpen

HARD AND RUTHLESS II

By Von Wiley Hall

LEVELS TO THIS SHYT II

By Ah'Million

MOB TIES III

By SayNoMore

BODYMORE MURDERLAND II

Money, Murder & Memories 3

By Delmont Player
THE LAST OF THE OGS III
Tranay Adams
FOR THE LOVE OF A BOSS II
By C. D. Blue

Available Now

RESTRAINING ORDER **I & II**
By **CA$H & Coffee**
LOVE KNOWS NO BOUNDARIES **I II & III**
By **Coffee**
RAISED AS A GOON I, II, III & IV
BRED BY THE SLUMS I, II, III
BLAST FOR ME I & II
ROTTEN TO THE CORE I II III
A BRONX TALE I, II, III
DUFFLE BAG CARTEL I II III IV V
HEARTLESS GOON I II III IV V
A SAVAGE DOPEBOY I II
DRUG LORDS I II III
CUTTHROAT MAFIA I II
By **Ghost**
LAY IT DOWN **I & II**
LAST OF A DYING BREED I II
BLOOD STAINS OF A SHOTTA I & II III

Malik D. Rice

By **Jamaica**
LOYAL TO THE GAME I II III
LIFE OF SIN I, II III
By **TJ & Jelissa**
BLOODY COMMAS I & II
SKI MASK CARTEL I II & III
KING OF NEW YORK I II,III IV V
RISE TO POWER I II III
COKE KINGS I II III IV
BORN HEARTLESS I II III IV
KING OF THE TRAP I II
By **T.J. Edwards**
IF LOVING HIM IS WRONG…I & II
LOVE ME EVEN WHEN IT HURTS I II III
By **Jelissa**
WHEN THE STREETS CLAP BACK I & II III
THE HEART OF A SAVAGE I II III
By **Jibril Williams**
A DISTINGUISHED THUG STOLE MY HEART I II & III
LOVE SHOULDN'T HURT I II III IV
RENEGADE BOYS I II III IV
PAID IN KARMA I II III
SAVAGE STORMS I II
By **Meesha**
A GANGSTER'S CODE I &, II III
A GANGSTER'S SYN I II III
THE SAVAGE LIFE I II III
CHAINED TO THE STREETS I II III
BLOOD ON THE MONEY I II

By J-Blunt

PUSH IT TO THE LIMIT

By **Bre' Hayes**

BLOOD OF A BOSS **I, II, III, IV, V**

SHADOWS OF THE GAME

TRAP BASTARD

By **Askari**

THE STREETS BLEED MURDER **I, II & III**

THE HEART OF A GANGSTA I II& III

By **Jerry Jackson**

CUM FOR ME I II III IV V VI VII

An **LDP Erotica Collaboration**

BRIDE OF A HUSTLA **I II & II**

THE FETTI GIRLS **I, II& III**

CORRUPTED BY A GANGSTA I, II III, IV

BLINDED BY HIS LOVE

THE PRICE YOU PAY FOR LOVE I II

DOPE GIRL MAGIC I II III

By **Destiny Skai**

WHEN A GOOD GIRL GOES BAD

By **Adrienne**

THE COST OF LOYALTY I II III

By Kweli

A GANGSTER'S REVENGE **I II III & IV**

THE BOSS MAN'S DAUGHTERS I II III IV V

A SAVAGE LOVE **I & II**

BAE BELONGS TO ME I II

A HUSTLER'S DECEIT I, II, III

WHAT BAD BITCHES DO I, II, III

173

SOUL OF A MONSTER I II III

KILL ZONE

A DOPE BOY'S QUEEN I II

By **Aryanna**

A KINGPIN'S AMBITON

A KINGPIN'S AMBITION **II**

I MURDER FOR THE DOUGH

By **Ambitious**

TRUE SAVAGE I II III IV V VI VII

DOPE BOY MAGIC I, II, III

MIDNIGHT CARTEL I II III

CITY OF KINGZ I II

By **Chris Green**

A DOPEBOY'S PRAYER

By **Eddie "Wolf" Lee**

THE KING CARTEL **I, II & III**

By **Frank Gresham**

THESE NIGGAS AIN'T LOYAL **I, II & III**

By **Nikki Tee**

GANGSTA SHYT **I II &III**

By **CATO**

THE ULTIMATE BETRAYAL

By **Phoenix**

BOSS'N UP **I , II & III**

By **Royal Nicole**

I LOVE YOU TO DEATH

By Destiny J

I RIDE FOR MY HITTA

I STILL RIDE FOR MY HITTA

By **Misty Holt**

LOVE & CHASIN' PAPER

By **Qay Crockett**

TO DIE IN VAIN

SINS OF A HUSTLA

By **ASAD**

BROOKLYN HUSTLAZ

By **Boogsy Morina**

BROOKLYN ON LOCK I & II

By **Sonovia**

GANGSTA CITY

By **Teddy Duke**

A DRUG KING AND HIS DIAMOND I & II III

A DOPEMAN'S RICHES

HER MAN, MINE'S TOO I, II

CASH MONEY HO'S

THE WIFEY I USED TO BE I II

By Nicole Goosby

TRAPHOUSE KING **I II & III**

KINGPIN KILLAZ I II III

STREET KINGS I II

PAID IN BLOOD **I II**

CARTEL KILLAZ I II III

DOPE GODS I II

By **Hood Rich**

LIPSTICK KILLAH **I, II, III**

CRIME OF PASSION I II & III

FRIEND OR FOE I II

By **Mimi**

Malik D. Rice

STEADY MOBBN' **I, II, III**

THE STREETS STAINED MY SOUL

By **Marcellus Allen**

WHO SHOT YA **I, II, III**

SON OF A DOPE FIEND I II

HEAVEN GOT A GHETTO

Renta

GORILLAZ IN THE BAY **I II III IV**

TEARS OF A GANGSTA I II

3X KRAZY I II

DE'KARI

TRIGGADALE I II III

Elijah R. Freeman

GOD BLESS THE TRAPPERS I, II, III

THESE SCANDALOUS STREETS I, II, III

FEAR MY GANGSTA I, II, III IV, V

THESE STREETS DON'T LOVE NOBODY I, II

BURY ME A G I, II, III, IV, V

A GANGSTA'S EMPIRE I, II, III, IV

THE DOPEMAN'S BODYGAURD I II

THE REALEST KILLAZ I II III

THE LAST OF THE OGS I II

Tranay Adams

THE STREETS ARE CALLING

Duquie Wilson

MARRIED TO A BOSS... I II III

By Destiny Skai & Chris Green

KINGZ OF THE GAME I II III IV V

Playa Ray

SLAUGHTER GANG I II III

RUTHLESS HEART I II III

By Willie Slaughter

FUK SHYT

By Blakk Diamond

DON'T F#CK WITH MY HEART I II

By Linnea

ADDICTED TO THE DRAMA I II III

IN THE ARM OF HIS BOSS II

By Jamila

YAYO I II III IV

A SHOOTER'S AMBITION I II

By S. Allen

TRAP GOD I II III

RICH $AVAGE

By Troublesome

FOREVER GANGSTA

GLOCKS ON SATIN SHEETS I II

By Adrian Dulan

TOE TAGZ I II III

LEVELS TO THIS SHYT

By Ah'Million

KINGPIN DREAMS I II III

By Paper Boi Rari

CONFESSIONS OF A GANGSTA I II III

By Nicholas Lock

I'M NOTHING WITHOUT HIS LOVE

SINS OF A THUG

TO THE THUG I LOVED BEFORE

Malik D. Rice

THE LIFE OF A HOOD STAR

By Ca$h & Rashia Wilson

THE STREETS WILL NEVER CLOSE

By K'ajji

CREAM I II

By Yolanda Moore

NIGHTMARES OF A HUSTLA I II

By King Dream

CONCRETE KILLAZ

By Kingpen

HARD AND RUTHLESS

By Von Wiley Hall

GHOST MOB II

Stilloan Robinson

MOB TIES I II

By SayNoMore

BODYMORE MURDERLAND

By Delmont Player

FOR THE LOVE OF A BOSS

By C. D. Blue

BOOKS BY LDP'S CEO, CA$H

TRUST IN NO MAN

TRUST IN NO MAN 2

TRUST IN NO MAN 3

BONDED BY BLOOD

SHORTY GOT A THUG

THUGS CRY

THUGS CRY 2

THUGS CRY 3

TRUST NO BITCH

TRUST NO BITCH 2

TRUST NO BITCH 3

TIL MY CASKET DROPS

RESTRAINING ORDER

RESTRAINING ORDER 2

IN LOVE WITH A CONVICT

LIFE OF A HOOD STAR

Money, Murder & Memories 3

CPSIA information can be obtained
at www.ICGtesting.com
Printed in the USA
LVHW012336290821
696386LV00018B/2519